How could Vince promise Tessa more than "now"?

How could he consider being the husband she needed when he'd failed at it once before? When he'd never had a role model to see how it should be done? Maybe that's what had kept him from staying twenty years ago. Maybe that's what kept him from moving them forward now. Tessa deserved someone who would put her first, romance her, court her, be steadfast and committed. He didn't know if he was capable of that.

For now he was committed to Sean, and that's all he knew.

Dear Reader,

What would we do without baby experts?

I remember bringing my son home from the hospital as a young wife and mother. Suddenly I realized my husband and I were embarking on an exciting but frightening adventure. This little baby would be in our keeping for a lifetime and we had responsibility for him 24/7. The first week I called his doctor twice, sought my mother and my mother-in-law's advice…and prayed I was making the right decisions.

My hero, Vince Rossi, unexpectedly becomes a dad overnight and returns to his hometown in Texas. Fortunately his former teenage bride, who he hasn't seen in twenty years, is a pediatrician. Tessa won't turn away any child and she becomes his baby expert.

Vince and Tessa's romance is the first book in my THE BABY EXPERTS trilogy. Readers can write to me at P.O. Box 1545, Hanover, PA 17331, or e-mail me through my Web site at www.karenrosesmith.com, for excerpts and the latest info.

All my best,

Karen Rose Smith

LULLABY
FOR TWO

KAREN ROSE SMITH

SPECIAL EDITION

Published by Silhouette Books

America's Publisher of Contemporary Romance

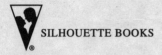

SILHOUETTE BOOKS

ISBN-13: 978-0-373-65443-7
ISBN-10:   0-373-65443-X

Recycling programs for this product may not exist in your area.

LULLABY FOR TWO

Books by Karen Rose Smith

KAREN ROSE SMITH

Award-winning and bestselling author Karen Rose Smith has seen more than sixty novels published since 1991. Living in Pennsylvania with her husband—who was her college sweetheart—and their two cats, she has been writing full-time since the start of her career. She enjoys researching and visiting the West and Southwest where this series of books is set. Readers can receive updates on Karen's latest releases and write to her through her Web site at www.karenrosesmith.com, or at P.O. Box 1545, Hanover, PA 17331.

To my mother, Romaine Arcuri Cacciola,
my mother-in-law, Rita Smith, and my husband's cousin
DeSales Sterner—my baby experts. Mom and Reet—
I miss you. Sis—my son's godmother and
my special friend—thanks for always being there.

AUTHOR NOTE

Adoption procedures may vary according to individual
circumstances, agencies and current state law.

Chapter One

Vince Rossi stood in shock in front of the receptionist's sliding-glass window.

He'd known he'd probably have to deal with his past at *some* point. But reading the third name on the placard beside the window, he knew that karma was ready to bite him in the butt today.

He studied the letters of Dr. Tessa McGuire's name as if somehow they'd change before his eyes. But they didn't. She was one of the pediatricians in this practice and he'd have to deal with it. He had a two-out-of-three chance of Sean's chart not landing in her stack. Those weren't bad odds.

The seven-month-old baby nestled in Vince's arm gurgled and stared up at him with sparkling blue eyes. Vince's heart melted just as it had from the moment he'd first held the little boy. Was it possible he'd become Sean's legal guardian only two and a half months ago? Only a week ago he'd returned to his hometown of Sagebrush, outside of Lubbock, Texas, in an attempt to find Sean the medical attention he needed, as well as put them both on the pathway to a new life. Vince had been impressed by the Family Tree Health Center where this pediatric practice as well as obstetrical, counseling, ophthalmological and a few other specialty practices were located.

The receptionist had finished her call and opened the glass window, staring at Vince expectantly.

"Sean Davidson's the patient, but I'm his legal guardian—Vince Rossi. Our appointment is for eleven-thirty," Vince said.

The woman checked off his name on the list in front of her. But before she could utter a word, the door to the waiting area opened.

Tessa McGuire appeared.

Her blond hair was still soft and wavy on her shoulders, her forget-me-not-blue eyes bright, her face mature in its beauty now. It had been twenty years since Vince had last seen her.

"Sean Davidson," she called cheerily. Then her gaze fell on Vince, recognized him, and her whole body went perfectly still.

Vince knew there was no use pretending. No point skirting the issue. Too much was at stake for Sean.

He strode forward and stopped in front of her. "I didn't know we'd be assigned to you. I'm Sean's legal guardian. If you'll have a problem treating him, I can find another doctor."

Tessa had always been the perfect lady, the well-bred daughter of one of the richest ranchers in Sagebrush. She was pale now, as if the shock of seeing Vince had affected her physically. He knew the feeling. Acid burned in his gut.

Sean wriggled in his arms and cooed, reminding Vince of

why he was here. He repositioned the baby in his arm, careful of Sean's injured shoulder.

Tessa was watching, missing nothing. Finally she spoke. "Treating Sean won't be a problem. Please follow me."

So polite. So proper. So ready to do what she thought was right.

She'd thought going home to her father was right…divorcing Vince was right…forgetting they'd ever been married was right.

He followed her, almost curious what the privacy of an examination room might reveal. His body was already warning him that twenty years hadn't made a difference in his attraction to her. Tessa McGuire had always turned him on more quickly than any other woman. Apparently, that hadn't changed.

Awkward silence settled over the small room.

Tessa was studying him as he mentally ticked off the differences she'd see. At thirty-eight, there were strands of gray in his black hair. A scar from an arrest-gone-bad marred his left jaw. After he'd left Sagebrush, Air Force conditioning had put muscles on his lean body. After that, a workout regimen had kept him conditioned as a homicide detective.

He gave them both a few seconds to absorb the shock of seeing each other again. Finally he asked, "Do you want Sean on the table?"

In this examination room, colorful cartoon characters walked and danced and played on the walls in artistically drawn murals. Sean was looking all around, fascinated by them.

In answer to Vince's question, Tessa took a few steps forward and stopped. "I'll take him." She reached for his son.

Vince thought of Sean as his son even though he hadn't

formally adopted him yet. He was waiting until they settled into a permanent place.

Transferring Sean to Tessa seemed to have an electric effect on them both. As her hands slid around the baby, they brushed Vince's chest. He caught a glimpse of startled awareness in Tessa's eyes as she tucked Sean into her arms, ducked her head and carried the little boy to the table.

Sean didn't seem to mind being held by her. He looked up at Tessa, waved his good arm and gurgled as if saying hello.

The expression on Tessa's face was so tender, so caring that Vince suddenly understood she'd become a pediatrician because while she'd never bear children of her own, in this specialty she could take care of everyone's kids.

As she settled Sean on the table, she asked, "How long have you been back in Sagebrush?"

"We drove in from Albuquerque last Monday."

Her gaze lifted to meet his. Then she quickly glanced away, concentrated on his baby again, took Sean's temperature with the ear thermometer, and offered him her finger— maybe to test his grip. After tickling his tummy, she warmed her stethoscope with her palm before slipping it under Sean's T-shirt.

Vince took the opportunity to study Tessa again. Under her white coat decorated with cartoon characters, she wore a light blue, silky blouse and navy skirt. Her navy shoes had a small heel, just high enough to delineate the curves of her legs. She was as slender as she'd been as a teenager, as slender as she'd been before she'd gotten pregnant.

Vince veered away from thoughts and memories he'd tamped down for a very long time.

After she finished listening to Sean's heart and lungs, she examined the rest of him, making a game of using the tongue depressor, gently looking into his ears with the otoscope, running her hands over his injured right shoulder and testing his range of motion.

Still concentrating on the baby, she told Vince, "I received Sean's chart this morning. With his name different from yours…" She stopped. "I have to admit I skimmed the front of the form and just paid attention to the medical facts. If I'd studied it more carefully, I would have noticed your name, too."

"Tessa, I meant it when I said I could go to another doctor."

Now she looked him straight in the eye. "I don't turn children away, Vince."

Not even when you don't want to be in the same room with their parents? He didn't ask the question aloud.

"We might only be in Sagebrush until Sean's shoulder problems are resolved," he explained, thinking that would relieve any anxiety she might have about Sean being her patient.

"A shoulder injury like Sean's is complex." Again her gaze met his unswervingly. "We usually see brachial plexus injuries when a baby gets stuck during the birthing process. In this case, with a seat belt causing the shoulder injury, we have a similar situation. How did you hear about Dr. Rafferty?"

"Sean's doctor in Albuquerque went to med school with him and said he's top-notch. When I researched him on the Internet, I saw he specialized in these surgeries. So coming to Lubbock seemed to be the best decision I could make. I want the best for Sean."

Although she hadn't asked, he decided to give her a bit more personal information. Maybe then she'd share some of her own. "For the past thirteen years I've been a homicide detective with the Albuquerque P.D."

Her gaze shot to his.

"After the Air Force, I wanted to do something that made

a difference." He paused and added, "I never imagined that when my partner and his wife designated me in their will to be their baby's legal guardian, a car accident would take their lives and change mine."

Tessa continued examining Sean as she absorbed that. "You're a single dad?"

Tessa's tone was distinctly removed. Was she just making conversation? Trying to find out about Sean's situation? Or was her inquiry more personal than that?

"I'm not married. I never have been." When Tessa's eyes flashed a few silver sparks, he added, "I mean, except for us. Military service and then a police officer's schedule were tough on relationships."

After much soul-searching, Vince had realized he'd joined the Air Force to forget about Tessa…to wipe her pregnancy and their marriage out of his mind. After the Air Force, he'd focused on becoming a detective and had never looked back. It was still too painful.

However, now with Tessa listening to his every word, he knew he'd be looking back all the while he was in Sagebrush. Would *she?* He was too aware of her. Was she just as aware of him?

"Did you get a job with the Lubbock P.D.?" she asked nonchalantly, as if it didn't matter.

That had been his intention, but then he'd found out about another position. "Do you remember Ryder Greystone?" Ryder had been one of their classmates in high school.

Tessa nodded.

"He's with the Lubbock P.D. and I called him. He said sure, they could use me, but it turns out Sagebrush's chief of police, Clinton Farmer, had a heart attack and took a leave of absence. The mayor was having a problem finding a temporary replacement. After recuperation from bypass surgery, Farmer intends to come back at the end of August. So I applied, had several long interviews over the phone and was appointed to the position."

"You're going to be chief of police in Sagebrush?" Her eyes were wide with her surprise.

"Don't tell me you're having trouble seeing me as a law-and-order kind of guy," he joked. Maybe if they took a light touch, seeing each other again would be easier.

Tessa's cheeks flushed. "Oh, it's not that. I guess I thought you'd be living in Lubbock rather than Sagebrush. But if you're chief of police—"

"I'm renting a one-story duplex on Whitehorse Road. What about you? Are you in Lubbock or living with your dad?" Walter McGuire would be in his late sixties now. Vince had seen a billboard advertising cutting horses from Arrowhead Ranch, so he guessed Tessa's dad was still hard at work building up a legacy for her.

At the mention of her father, Tessa went quiet, readjusted Sean's clothes so they were back in place, then scooped him up off the table. "I'm sharing a house in Sagebrush with two friends."

Her tone seemed to say, *Not that it's any of your business.* His mention of her father had put her on the defensive. He should have known better.

"Sean looks healthy, other than his shoulder, of course," she assured Vince. "His chart says he has an appointment with Dr. Rafferty on June twelfth. If Dr. Rafferty believes surgery is not in order, then what are you going to do?"

"I'll serve as chief of police until Farmer comes back, then maybe return to Albuquerque. Everything's up in the air right now, Tessa. I'm just taking one day at a time."

At the sound of her first name on his lips, her body seemed to stiffen, her shoulders becoming a little squarer. Then she was handing Sean over to Vince, this time very careful not to touch him. The awkwardness in accomplishing that emphasized the relationship they'd once had and the lack of even friendship between them now.

To cover her attempt to stay distant from him, if not his baby, Tessa asked, "So you're exercising Sean's arm every day?"

"Yes. And the woman I've hired to take care of him knows how to do it, too."

Even as a teenager, Tessa had foregone perfume for more natural scents like fruity shampoos and lotions. Vince inhaled a hint of vanilla and strawberries that took him straight back to necking sessions with her in his beat-up pickup.

She crossed to the door and opened it. "Good luck with Dr. Rafferty. Make sure he sends me a report." Her expression softened a little. "I know what a stress this must be…to be worrying about Sean."

Their eyes locked and his heart pounded as he approached the doorway where she stood. Tessa pulled her gaze from his and touched Sean's hand. The baby took hold of her finger and looked up at her with seven-month-old fascination.

Vince knew exactly how his son felt.

Tessa removed her finger from Sean's fist. "Good luck, little one," she murmured.

After Vince gave her a nod and a muttered, "Thanks," he held Sean a little tighter and walked down the hall. How often had Tessa said those words before? How often had she looked at a baby and thought about her own? How often had she thought of *him* and blamed him for the hysterectomy she'd had no choice in having?

He might never know the answer. He and Tessa had been finished long ago. She obviously wanted to keep it that way.

Tessa hurried through the lobby of the Family Tree Health Center, hardly aware of the bright sunshine pouring in the plate-glass windows, barely noticing the photographs of children, moms and dads and families hung in casual to formal frames on the pale yellow walls. She was in a daze as she veered toward the coffee shop to the right of the main entrance, passed the bird-of-paradise potted plant and a ledge lined with pothos ivy.

Stopping to gain her focus again, she spotted the table where Emily Diaz and Francesca Talbot were sitting. She was late meeting them for lunch…late pulling herself to-gether…late trying to push the image of Vince's face out of her head…late trying not to remember the feel of baby Sean in her arms.

Vincent Rossi was back in Sagebrush and she was just going to have to deal with it.

Masterful at hiding what she didn't want others to see, she'd found she could let her guard down with Emily and Francesca. The three of them not only lived in a refurbished Victorian together but had become best friends.

Francesca greeted her first, sleek chestnut hair slipping over her shoulder, her green eyes sparkling as she beckoned Tessa toward their table. A neonatologist, Francesca had her office on the second floor of the center. She had office hours all day Monday, but spent most of her time at the hospital with her tiny patients.

Emily Diaz's big brown eyes were already studying Tessa as she approached the table. Emily had pulled her curly black hair back from her face and fastened it with a navy scrunchie.

Wearing Dr. Madison's staff smock—Emily was his obstetrical nurse—she could fade into the background if she wanted to and usually *did* want to. Tessa still didn't know why. Emily had only lived with her and Francesca for five months, but the empathetic way she had of listening had endeared her to both of them. Although Tessa realized they didn't know her whole story yet, she didn't push. Emily would tell them in time.

"We ordered the grilled-chicken salad for you and the peach iced tea. Is that okay?" Francesca asked.

They were usually short on time and both Emily and Francesca knew Tessa always ordered the same lunch.

"That's fine," she assured her with a distracted wave of her hand, taking her seat and dropping her purse to the floor.

"Rough morning?" Francesca asked.

Was it so obvious? Was she pale? Did the strain show? Had Vince realized how he had affected her?

Slipping the lemon slice off the side of her water glass, she squeezed it then dropped it in. After taking a few sips, she made sure that when she breathed in and then out it was deep and even.

"What happened?" Emily asked her, her concern obvious. "Problems with a patient?"

Tessa never discussed specifics about her patients and both women knew that. They were bound by the same terms of confidentiality. But they could talk in general terms.

"No, not a patient," Tessa replied quietly.

Her friends waited expectantly.

Tessa glanced around and saw that at their corner table they had relative privacy. "A ghost from my past walked into my office today." That was all she could say. Although Vince wasn't her patient, his son, Sean, was.

After exchanging a look with Emily, Francesca asked, "Not Vince Rossi?"

Because Tessa had lived with Francesca since her return to Sagebrush from California two years ago, the neonatologist had known Tessa's story. On the other hand, Emily, who had lived in Corpus Christi all of her life until her recent move to Sagebrush, only knew Tessa had had a hysterectomy, not the whole story behind it. It wasn't that Tessa hadn't wanted to confide in Emily, she just hadn't wanted to dredge it all up again. The hysterectomy had affected her life and still affected it now. She'd discussed it with her two friends when she'd decided to apply to become an adoptive parent, but not why or how it had happened.

"Who's Vince Rossi?" Emily asked.

Tessa dropped her chin into her hands, rubbed her face, pushed back her hair and realized it was time Emily knew her history, too. Maybe excavating the hurt would remind her to stay away from Vince.

Of course she'd stay away from Vince! Once his little boy's surgery was over, he'd be gone. That was Vince. He *left*.

After taking another sip of water, Tessa explained, "Vince and I met in high school." Saying those words brought it all back…back to that morning in the library during her senior year when she'd been sitting in a far corner out of the way and hadn't been able to keep her tears from falling.

She hadn't known Vince well. He'd taken vo-tech courses and she'd taken academic preparation. She'd attended a private girls' school until ninth grade, then had made a deal with her father. She'd go to any college he chose, if he'd let her attend public high school.

So there she was, tears falling down her face, when a deep voice at her side asked, "Are you okay?"

Vince Rossi was everything she shouldn't have been attracted to, with his dark, handsome looks and brooding gray eyes, his wrong-side-of-the-tracks attitude. With few flirting skills and little experience, she'd been afraid to get close to him.

"I'm fine," she'd told him, but her tears stated a different story.

He sat down beside her. "You don't look fine."

Back then she didn't have close friends because her father had still controlled her life, her comings and goings and who she could bring to the house. Female classmates cut her out of their cliques. She was an outsider who couldn't break into groups with friendships established since grade school. A couple of girls who did befriend her only tried because of her father's wealth and what they could enjoy because of it. It hadn't taken her long to catch on.

So because of all that, because she felt alone much of the time, she'd told Vince the truth. "We had to put my dog to sleep. He was my best friend and he had a stroke. I miss him so much."

Vince's expression had reflected kindness and her own sadness. "I know what it's like to miss someone. My mom left when I was a kid."

"My mom died when I was born," she'd replied softly.

They'd gazed into each other's eyes, and she'd fallen in love with Vincent Rossi right then and there.

"Tessa?" Francesca called her name, bringing her back to the present.

"Oh, I'm sorry, I—" She took a breath and moved her fork. "Vince and I connected. We more than connected." She sighed. "Then I got pregnant that April. We waited until after graduation to tell my dad. Vince insisted on marrying me, so my dad disowned me."

"You can't be serious!" Emily knew Tessa and her dad were close now.

"Oh, I'm very serious. Vince insisted on doing the right thing and married me. He got a job as a roofer during the day and worked in a saddlemaker's shop at night. I hardly saw him. I was pretty sick throughout my pregnancy. I worked at Thelma's Dress Shop. When I couldn't be on the sales floor, I helped her with bookkeeping."

"Thelma's? Over on Tumbleweed? It's been there that long?" Emily asked.

Francesca answered her. "Thelma's daughter runs it now. But Thelma still comes in a few days a week."

"Go on," Emily encouraged Tessa. "I didn't mean to interrupt."

"Sometimes I forget you haven't lived here all your life," Tessa admitted. She was actually glad for Emily's interruption because what came next was the difficult part.

Francesca reached across the table and patted Tessa's hand. "It might be good to talk about it. You never do."

No, she never did…because she just wanted to forget. "I was twenty-six weeks pregnant when I went into labor. I had a placenta accreta. The placenta pulled a hole in my uterus and I hemorrhaged. We lost the baby and I had to have a hysterectomy."

Emily went very quiet. She brought her hands together in her lap, looked down at them and then returned her gaze to Tessa's. "I'm so very sorry, Tessa. That would be devastating for any woman. As a teenager, I can't even imagine what that did to you."

"When my father heard what happened, he blamed Vince and the life we were living. We had a walk-up apartment and the bare necessities. Everything we earned went for expenses and the baby. The night I went into labor, I collapsed and couldn't get to the phone. Our landlady found me and called the ambulance. I needed Vince but he wasn't there…he was working. When I was released, I made the choice to go home with Dad rather than back to our apartment. I didn't want to be a burden on Vince. I didn't know if he married me because he had to, or because he thought we were meant to be together, like I did."

She stopped to take a much-needed pause, then went on. "Vince…Vince came to my dad's. He told me the pregnancy and our marriage was a mistake, that we'd been too young. He knew I wanted to be a doctor and he said that's what I should be. He was going to join the Air Force, maybe make a career of it like his uncle had. His uncle was very different from his dad. His dad drank and couldn't hold a job, and I think Vince just needed to prove he was different, that he could succeed at something. He didn't ask me what *I* wanted. I could see he wasn't willing to fight for what we had."

"You were both grieving. You'd lost a child," Emily sympathized.

"A baby boy," Tessa murmured, her own voice catching. Then she regained her composure. "I know now no one should make major decisions about their life under those circumstances. But we did. He left, and I went to Stanford. Less than a year later I heard he was seeing someone. So I knew our relationship hadn't meant as much to him as it had to me. Even though we'd broken up, even though we'd gotten a divorce, I still felt betrayed."

"So what happened today?" Francesca prompted. "Why was he at your office? He's moved back and he has children?"

"I can't say. You know that. If you find out about Vince from someone else, that's fine. But I can't tell you anything more."

Francesca and Emily exchanged another of those looks, and Tessa knew what that meant. Sagebrush was a small town. They'd soon know *exactly* why Vincent Rossi had returned.

The waitress appeared, carrying a tray with their lunches. Tessa had no appetite whatsoever. However, she was determined that Vince Rossi's return would not affect her life. He would not turn her world upside down a second time.

Vince entered Sagebrush High School ten days later, cell phone to his ear. "Is everything okay?" he asked the woman he'd hired to take care of Sean.

"Just fine, Mr. Rossi. Sean ate all of his supper. I'm going to give him a bath and put him to bed. Or do you want me to keep him up until you come home?"

Vince had interviewed three women to watch Sean during his working hours. He'd liked Mrs. Zappa the best. She was a widow, a retired teacher who was available whenever he might need her and she loved kids. Almost everyone in town knew her and they'd all given her good references. So he shouldn't worry when he was away from Sean. But he'd been caring for the little boy day and night, all by himself, since the beginning of March. It was hard to let go.

"No, don't keep him up," he directed her. "He'll just get cranky. If he wakes up later, I'll read him a story and then put him down again. I should be home by nine…ten at the latest. The parent meeting will probably last about a half hour, and then there will be questions and answers afterward."

He knew Tessa was going to be at the meeting, too. At least this time he'd be prepared to see her. This time he was ready.

That's what he told himself.

Until he walked into the principal's office and saw her. She was standing at the counter where visitors signed in and out, where students made their needs and wants known. She was wearing a raspberry-colored suit with a cream blouse and looked like ten million bucks.

She must have heard him come in because she turned, and their gazes collided. "Vince," she said in acknowledgment, her soft voice running up his spine like a sensual finger. "I thought you might send one of your officers to take care of this."

Maybe she was *hoping* he'd send one of his officers to speak. Then she wouldn't have to see him. "I thought tonight was too important to skip. I don't think parents realize exactly what dangers crop up around the prom and the summer holidays. They need to know what to do to talk to their kids and protect them."

Tessa gave him a long, studying assessment. "I agree. The principal said you were going to talk first. Do you have a prepared presentation?"

He grinned at her. "Nope. I'm going to wing it." Then he shrugged. "I've done this before about a thousand times. It's all in my head."

She lifted her zippered portfolio. "It's all in my notes."

He laughed. That was Tessa, always organized and prepared. He took a few steps closer to her and his laugh faded. "Are you going to cover alcohol and drugs?"

She didn't step back, just nodded.

Her blond brows were so delicately shaped. Her fringe of lashes was darker than her hair. Her blue eyes had always been guileless. He could smell vanilla and strawberries again, and he saw the pulse at her neck beating.

"Are you nervous about this?" he asked.

"The presentation? Or giving the presentation with you?"

"Either. Both."

"I'm not seventeen anymore. I don't get nervous as easily."

The bravado was new, as was her confidence level. But so much was the same.

He gently placed a finger on the pulse point of her neck and could feel exactly how fast her heart was beating. "You're nervous about *something*," he insisted.

She could have slapped his hand away, which was sort of what he expected. She definitely could have backed away. But she just stood there, gazing into his eyes, and he realized that was worse than shutting him out.

Because he saw the pain he'd caused Tessa…and now he knew she'd never forgive him.

Chapter Two

"I see the two of you have met," said Joe Mercer, the principal of Sagebrush High School, to Tessa and Vince as he exited his private office.

Tessa didn't speak. She still felt breathless and disconcerted from Vince's touch.

"We went to school here together," Vince filled in when the silence grew awkward.

Joe, a handsome man in his midforties and prematurely gray, asked Tessa, "Is the school the same as you remembered it?"

Walking into Sagebrush High brought back too many memories as far as she was concerned. Although she'd convinced her father to let her attend the public high school, she'd felt alone and very much the outsider here—until Vince had dropped into her life. "It's the same. Though the halls have a new coat of paint and the auditorium was added on since I…we…came to school here."

As she glanced at Vince, she saw his eyes had turned a stormy gray. Was he remembering the kisses they'd shared behind locker doors? The quick hugs before a test? The after-school rendezvous in his pickup truck in the parking lot? She might not want those memories to still be intact, but in spite of her best effort to tame or banish them, they were. The deepening of lines on Vince's brow told her he couldn't banish them, either.

She purposefully glanced at her watch. "I suppose the parents will be gathering. Are we speaking to them in the auditorium?"

"Unfortunately we won't have enough parents here to need the auditorium," Joe replied. "They think they know their kids so most don't attend these meetings. We're gathering in the library."

As the principal motioned for Tessa to precede him into the hall, Vince asked him, "You publicized this?"

"Absolutely. Flyers went home with the kids. We posted it on our Web site. There was even a notice in the paper."

Vince had come up beside Tessa, his long-legged stride easily taking him ahead of her. When he realized it, he slowed.

Just looking at him could still make her giddy. At eighteen, he'd been most girls' fantasy date, with his good looks, sexy beard stubble and broad shoulders that could make a girl feel safe. At thirty-eight, he was so much more. The lines etched around his eyes had come from maturity and experience. She guessed his strong jaw still carried a shadowed beard line after five o'clock. But tonight he was clean-shaven, ready for his part of the program.

She tried not to look too hard or see too much, but in spite of herself, she noticed that tonight he wore a denim blazer, white oxford shirt and black jeans, a broad-rimmed cowboy hat low over his eyes. He'd obviously kept in shape. She'd been able to tell that from the muscles evident under his polo shirt that day in her office. She'd tried to ignore the changes in his body as he'd handed Sean to her…as he'd loomed in the room while she'd examined his son.

His son.

"How is Sean adjusting to the move?" she asked, as their footsteps echoed in the hall and they drew closer to the library.

"Probably better than I am," Vince admitted with a rueful smile.

She'd be safer not commenting on Vince's adjustment. "If Sean's sleeping, eating well and seems happy, then he's adjusting."

"Sometimes he wakes up around 2:00 a.m. and wants to play. I walk him for a while and talk to him, then he settles down again."

She didn't know why she was having such a difficult time imagining Vince with the baby, accepting full care of him. Maybe because while she was pregnant he simply hadn't been around much and she'd wished he had been.

As they entered the library, Tessa noticed that most of the rectangular tables for eight were filled, and about a hundred parents had gathered.

Joe led them to the circulation desk. A podium was positioned in front of it with two chairs by its side.

"I didn't want this to be too formal," he told them in a low voice. "If we can keep the meeting more conversational, give parents a chance to ask questions and not feel a barrier between you and them, that would be best. Chief Rossi, after my opening remarks I'll introduce you. Is there anything I need to set up for you? A bit of a background?"

"I'll include my background when I talk to them," Vince assured the principal.

"The same for you, Dr. McGuire?" Joe asked.

She nodded, eager to hear what Vince had to say. In spite of herself she was curious about where he'd been and what he'd done over the past twenty years. Not that he would go into all of that publicly. But she might get a hint.

She was always all nerves before she gave a presentation. She was much better one-on-one, or in a small group. But she did it as a challenge, as she did everything. If she was afraid of something, she knew she had to walk straight toward it and face it. Was that how Vince ran his life, too?

She sensed a confidence about him that had been lacking when he was a teenager. At eighteen he'd stood tall and said what he thought more because of defiance than confidence.

Now, however, he walked up to the podium and gave the group a relaxed smile. After he swiped off his Stetson, he laid it on the counter behind him and ran a hand through his thick black hair.

"I'm Vince Rossi, chief of police of the Sagebrush P.D." He nodded to the group. "It's good to see all of you here. I know you're wondering what *I* can tell you about your sons and daughters. Maybe nothing. Maybe something. Maybe my experience in law enforcement will tell you the pitfalls available to teenagers in a small town, especially when drugs, alcohol and vehicles are involved. If you listen to what I have to say, I promise to answer each and every one of your questions, even if I'm here all night."

Whether Vince had had psychological training in the method he used to approach the group, Tessa didn't know. But what he'd said had worked. All gazes were on him.

They were attentive, thanks to the promise of individual attention if they needed it. Vince already held them in the palm of his hand.

Unbidden, she thought about his palm. How it had touched her in pleasure and gentleness and teasing. Taking a deep breath, she looked down at the portfolio on her lap rather than at Vince. She'd be better off concentrating on his words than on him.

Tessa's approach, when it was her turn, was altogether different from Vince's. She spoke as a friend of the family, warning of signs of changes in their children's personalities, explaining that no child was immune from peer pressure and the need for friends' approval. After she finished, she assured them she'd also be available to speak to any parent who had concerns.

During the next hour both she and Vince answered questions, gave advice, but mostly listened.

When only a dozen or so parents remained, talking among themselves in small groups, Vince crossed to her. "I'm going to have to face their concerns in another thirteen or fourteen years." He shook his head. "That makes me want to bury my head in the sand."

When they'd separated, Vince had buried his head in the sand where *she* was concerned...where their marriage was concerned. He hadn't wanted to see how much she loved him...how much she wanted their marriage to work...how sad she was because of the loss of their child. It had been easier for him to walk away.

All these years she'd put the past in a compartment that she'd shut tight. She couldn't seem to do that tonight, but she was giving it her best shot. She reminded herself just to treat this evening as a professional, not as Vince's ex-wife. "Drugs and alcohol don't have to be a rite of passage."

After their gazes met for a few long moments, Vince remarked, "It's a shame you're a pediatrician."

"Why?"

"Because these parents would all put their kids in your care if you didn't just treat babies. How long have you been back here?"

"Two years. Since Family Tree opened."

Suddenly, one of the men who appeared to be a few years older than Vince broke away from another couple and approached Tessa. "Dr. McGuire, I'm Tim Daltry. I know your dad pretty well. He's letting my son, Ray, work at the ranch after school and weekends to make money for college. Just wanted to let you know how grateful I am for that. He's paying Ray real good and it's going to make a difference."

Tessa had always admired her father's generosity. He wasn't public about it, but he did things like this when he could. "If Dad hired your son, I'm sure Ray's giving him a good day's work for what he's getting."

Always aware of Vince even when she didn't want to be, she noticed his mouth had gone tight at the mention of her father. She wondered just how deep his resentment ran. She'd had to let go of hers. Everything her father had done had stemmed from his love for her. And although at the time she hadn't agreed with any of it, her father in essence had proved himself right—because Vince *had* left. He'd abandoned her to find a life that suited him better.

"Well, I just wanted to introduce myself," Daltry said. "Give your dad my regards." His gaze went to Vince. "You gave us a lot to think about. I can't quite see Chief Farmer ever speaking to a group like this."

"I wouldn't know," Vince replied casually. "But Chief

Farmer *is* planning to come back as soon as he's recovered. If you want to do more programs like this, you could make the suggestion."

"Maybe I will. Rumor has it you were a homicide detective in Albuquerque. Is that true?"

"Sure is."

"What made you come to a town like Sagebrush?"

Tessa could see Daltry was wondering if Vince had gotten into trouble somehow, or been demoted, or been kicked off the force. Everyone liked meaty gossip. She and Vince had been the butt of it twenty years ago. But that had been a long time ago. Some people might remember, others might not. Since she'd returned to Sagebrush, residents here had respected her privacy. But now that Vince was back...

To her surprise, Vince didn't clam up but was completely forthright with Daltry. "My life changed. I'm a father now, and a homicide detective's life wasn't conducive to bringing up a child."

"But if you're only here for a few months..." Daltry trailed off.

"I'm just concentrating on what I have to do here, then I'll look past that."

It was a smooth answer and one that didn't tell Tessa anything. Would Vince consider staying in the area? *Would* he go back to Albuquerque or on to somewhere new? She could easily see that happening.

Mr. Daltry bid them both good-night and followed a few other parents out of the library.

Vince looked over at the principal, who was talking to one lingering parent. Then he checked his watch. "I know it's getting late and we'll both be up early, but how would you like to grab a cup of coffee at the diner?"

She couldn't read his expression or tell anything from his eyes, so she decided to just honestly ask, "Why?"

After studying her for a long moment, he replied, "Because there's ice between us and I'd like to chip at it a little."

He was right. She'd thought she'd put the past in the past. But seeing Vince again stirred up old feelings—feelings she'd thought she'd dealt with, feelings that had no place in her life now. If he was going to be in Sagebrush and she was going to run into him, she didn't want those feelings disrupting her existence. Sure, she had walls up. She'd admit that. But a tête-à-tête with Vince? Sitting across the table from him, gazing into those steel-gray eyes...

Would that make matters better or worse?

For better or worse, for richer or poorer...

Those vows had meant nothing to him. But she didn't want to hate him. She didn't want to resent him. She didn't want to be bitter about what had happened back then. She didn't want a squall of memories to assault her just from standing close to him.

Closure was what she needed. Facing what she didn't want to face might do the trick.

"I have time for a cup of...tea," she substituted. They both used to like rich, dark coffee—decaf for her after she was pregnant—no sugar, no cream. Especially in the morning after making love...

She had shut down memories for years. But tonight she might have to let them rise to the surface so she could move on...so she could prove to herself she was over Vince Rossi for good.

The end-of-May night was wonderfully clear with a bright half-moon and thousands of stars twinkling as Tessa walked beside Vince to the diner. So many stars, so many wishes. She'd stopped wishing on stars when she was eighteen and her dreams had crashed.

Awkward silence wrapped around them with neither of them knowing what to say.

"So much for ice breaking," Vince said wryly as they approached the diner with its flashing neon sign announcing to the world that the Yellow Rose Diner was open.

"We used to know each other, Vince. We don't anymore. That's why it's hard to talk."

He stopped before the glass door and didn't attempt to pull it open. "Are you telling me a former homicide detective and a doctor have nothing in common? We're *people,* Tessa. If you pretend I'm a stranger you met at a party, I'll bet then you'd have something to say."

"Meaning?" She could feel herself bristling and knew they were off to a difficult start.

Vince blew out a breath. "Meaning you handled that crowd—most of them strangers—tonight like a pro. You didn't have difficulty speaking to anyone who approached you. So why is it so hard to have a conversation with *me?*"

There were a thousand answers in her head, beginning with *because you left, because you abandoned me, because you didn't stand up to my father, because you thought I wasn't worth a fight.* But silence seemed to be her best recourse and she stuck to it.

If he'd continued to challenge her, they might have walked away from each other right then and there. But instead of being oppositional, he murmured gently, "Tessa."

The sound of her name in just that way twisted her heart. She confided, "I guess maybe there's too much to say and I'm afraid the wrong thing will spill out. I don't want to say anything I'll regret. And let's face it, we never just talked about the weather."

Now when she gazed into his eyes, his were conflicted with memories of everything they'd shared years ago—from dreams and plans to marriage and hopes for their baby.

Breaking eye contact, he opened the door to the diner.

The restaurant was empty but Tessa recognized the waitress wiping down the red counter. "Hi, Mindy."

"Dr. McGuire! I haven't seen you for a while." She cast an assessing glance at Vince, then screwed up her face into an I-think-I-know-you look. "Aren't you the new chief of police? Rossi, isn't it? Aren't you originally from Sagebrush?" She glanced quickly at Tessa and Tessa wondered if Mindy knew their story. But Mindy went on, addressing Vince again. "Dusty was telling me the guys were all nervous when they heard you were coming back, being a homicide detective and all. But he said you weren't trying to make a whole bunch of changes and you seemed like a right nice guy."

Vince's complexion grew a little ruddier. Instead of commenting on what the waitress had said, he motioned to the glass-covered cake dish with its three doughnuts. "So this is where Dusty buys the doughnuts. They're always gone ten minutes after he brings them in."

Mindy smiled. "We've got the best baked goods in town. I've got half an apple pie left and you and Doc McGuire deserve a piece."

She whispered in an aside to Vince, throwing her chin at Tessa, "The doc gives me samples for my boy when he's sick, so I can stretch my tips a little further." Motioning to the table back in the corner, she suggested, "If you two want some privacy, you can have the best table in the house. Tea for you, Doc?"

Tessa nodded.

"Black coffee for you, Chief?"

"How did you know?"

"Just a guess. You look like the type. Just made a new pot."

Vince waited until Tessa was seated, then pulled out his own chair. After he sat across from her, he shook his head ruefully. "I'd forgotten everyone in this town knows everything about everyone else."

"You're a public figure."

"Not for long."

He was leaving. She had to remember that.

Swiping off his Stetson, he settled it on one of the chairs. "When I brought Sean in to see you, I forgot to ask for a recommendation for a physical therapist. It's another two weeks until we see Dr. Rafferty and I want to make sure the exercises I'm doing with him are enough."

"Unfortunately there aren't any physical therapy practices in Sagebrush. You'll have to go to Lubbock."

"I'll go wherever I need to go."

She saw that he would. "I know several good therapists, but let me ask around and I'll find out who's best with a child Sean's age."

"I'd appreciate that."

Mindy brought their drinks and pie.

Tessa picked up her fork and took a bite, rolling her eyes in obvious pleasure. "This makes up for not eating supper."

"Did you work late?"

"I always work late. It depends on how long rounds at the hospital take, if I have an emergency, if there's a problem patient who runs overtime. There are never enough hours in a day."

They ate in silence for a few moments until Vince asked, "So your dad still raises cutting horses?"

She hadn't expected the subject of her father to come up again so soon. "He does. He has a manager and a trainer, so he doesn't do as much of the training as he used to. But he pushes himself to stay moving so his arthritis doesn't get the best of him." She took another bite of her pie, though her stomach was churning. "But that isn't really what you wanted to know, is it? If you want to ask me about him, go ahead."

He eyed her assessingly. "Does he still control your life?"

Was that what Vince had always thought?

He'd never really understood her relationship with her father. But she wasn't going to be able to explain it to him over a ten-minute cup of tea. He'd never gotten to know her dad and that had always been part of the problem.

Her father had been protective of her when she was a teenager, afraid Vince would ruin her life. That's why he'd been opposed to them dating. When they'd married, he'd disowned her, hoping that would bring her to her senses. Instead she'd held on to Vince and the life they could have. Until she'd lost the baby.

A protective urge rose up in her—the urge to protect her dad and to protect herself. It was close to anger, close to re-belliousness, close to all the words she'd never been able to say to Vince because he'd left and hadn't wanted to hear them. "You said you wanted to chip at the ice walls between us. I don't think this is the way to do it."

He leaned away from the table in obvious frustration. "I don't know how else to say it, Tessa."

She saw he was being sincere. She matched that sincerity with the truth. "My dad and I are close, but we have separate lives. He respects the decisions I make."

"Did he ask you to come back to Sagebrush?"

She'd never had a short fuse. In fact, she'd always thought

she'd been blessed with an overabundance of the gift of patience. But Vince had always made her question herself and her feelings, what she thought and what she believed. She reacted more strongly whenever she was around him, to him and to everyone else.

She tried to keep her voice steady. "Actually, he didn't want me to come home. He didn't think that was good for my career. But he got tossed by a two-year-old horse he was trying to gentle and broke his arm. He could manage. He had help. But when I came home to visit, I could see how he was slowing down. I'd been so focused on med school and residency, my visits had been brief. I took a good look at my life in California and didn't feel particularly attached. When I heard about the Family Tree Health Center opening, I decided to take the opportunity to come back. Does that answer your question?"

"Not exactly."

She laid her fork down, most of her pie uneaten. "Well, it's going to have to do." She picked up her purse and portfolio. "I'd better be going."

Vince stood, too.

"You can finish."

"I'm not letting you walk back to your car alone."

"This is Sagebrush, Vince."

"Yes, and I'm the chief of police. I know what goes on here." He took some bills from his wallet and laid them on the table.

She was going to protest, say she'd pay her half, but the look on his face told her just to head for the door. After a wave at Mindy, she pushed outside. A second later Vince was beside her, silent, not brooding, but definitely pensive.

After half a block he asked, "Did you miss anything about Sagebrush when you were gone?"

A glance at him told her that was a serious question. "I missed the ranch—the horses and cats, and particularly the smells. You know, old wood, saddle leather, sage, brush, the sun heating the damp grass. Mostly I missed riding."

"You couldn't find a stable in California?"

"Oh, sure. I went riding a few times. But it wasn't the same and I simply didn't have the time. After my shifts, I was dead on my feet. I snatched sleep when I could, studied, and didn't have much of a life outside of work."

"Were you in a pediatrics practice out there?"

"After my residency. I also volunteered at a free clinic. But I knew I'd burn out if I kept working at that pace."

They walked another half block without speaking. Tessa, curious about the path Vince had taken, asked, "Did your law enforcement interest begin in the service?"

"I was stationed at Kirkland Air Force Base in Albuquerque all four years because I was in law enforcement."

"But why the interest in the first place?"

There was a very long pause before Vince answered, "You knew my mother left. What you didn't know was that she was murdered."

Tessa stopped walking and turned to him, her hand on his arm. "Vince. I'm so sorry. You never said anything—"

"It wasn't something I wanted to remember or talk about. Still don't, really. She left me and my dad, went to New Orleans and was murdered by a lover. That's the long and short of it. So I guess I felt I was doing something to right what had gone wrong. That's not rational of course, but it led me where I am."

She could feel his taut muscles under his blazer. In the glow of the streetlamp, she could see a beard shadow darkening his jaw. What she couldn't see was the expression in his eyes under the brim of the Stetson that shadowed them.

Even so, due to her imagination or not, she could feel heat emanating from him, rising up from her, and currents rushing from her body into his and back again. She let go of his arm.

They began walking again and soon reached the school's parking lot where their cars were the only two left. His was a silver SUV. Hers was a small blue sedan. They were both in the front line of the lot about ten spaces apart.

He kept pace with her as she walked toward her car.

"I'm fine now," she assured him. "You can keep me in your sight as I get in and drive away."

"I will."

When he clasped her shoulder, she felt…fire. A rush of memories overwhelmed her. She would have backed away from them if she could have and from him. But his magnetic pull was too great to break.

"What's wrong?" he asked, though she suspected he knew.

"We're not strangers," she murmured, knowing that definitely wasn't the answer to his question.

"No, we're not. And even if we wanted to be, that wouldn't change what we were to each other."

What were we? a little voice inside her head screamed. Yet, no matter what his answer was, it was too late. They were over. They'd been over for a long time.

"You look scared." Vince's hand moved from her shoulder and tucked a strand of hair behind her ear. "Do I still have the power to move you?"

Now she did force herself to back away from his touch…forced herself to remember the sadness, the grief and the loss. "It would be foolish of me to answer that question."

Yet she knew by saying it, she already had.

Her keys in hand, she hurriedly pressed the remote and the car beeped at her. She opened the driver's door, slipped inside and quickly shut it. She didn't roll down her window. Maybe she was being a coward, but she didn't want to hear anything else Vince might have to say. She certainly didn't want him to touch her again because he *did* still move her and she couldn't accept that. She *wouldn't* accept that.

He stood there watching her as she backed up and drove faster than she should have out of the parking lot. She didn't glance into her rearview mirror.

She wouldn't look back again tonight. She absolutely wouldn't.

Chapter Three

A warning voice inside Tessa's head whispered, *You could have called Vince instead of showing up on the police department's doorstep*. She stood in front of the yellow stucco building, uncertain about being here. But she'd told Vince she'd recommend a physical therapist to him and that's what she was going to do.

The Sagebrush police department's heavy glass door led into a building that was old, almost as old as the town, with thick adobe walls and wide windowsills. The plank flooring was dull from years of foot traffic. The dispatcher sat at a scarred wood desk to the left. To the right, the receptionist, Ginny Ruja, busily tapped keyboard keys. The rest of the room was partitioned off by a wooden fence with a swinging gate at its center. There were three desks with computers, two of them occupied by officers in blue uniforms. Beyond the desk area, a hallway led to the left and the jail. To the right, Tessa glimpsed a closed door. It was probably Vince's office.

Crossing to the receptionist's desk, she smiled at Ginny, who brought her four-year-old son, Jeremy, to Tessa's practice.

Ginny looked up from her keyboard, and when she saw Tessa, her face was puzzled. "Hello, Dr. McGuire. Is something wrong? I hope you didn't have your purse stolen or anything like that."

Since this was Tessa's day off, she'd walked to the police station, merely slipping her keys into her jeans pocket. She'd intended to go for a brisk walk after she was finished here.

"Nothing's wrong." Even though Tessa knew Ginny, she felt awkward being here. The dispatcher and two officers were casting their gazes her way. "Is Vince Rossi in?" she asked.

Ginny's eyes widened in surprise. "The chief? Yes, he is, but he asked me not to disturb him for an hour so he could finish some paperwork." Ginny looked torn as to what she should do.

Tessa was disappointed, but she should have called before coming, anyway. She wasn't going to barge in when she didn't even belong here.

"I understand. I should have made an appointment." She slipped a folded index card from her pocket. "I told V— Chief Rossi that I would find some information he wanted." She held out the index card to Ginny. "If you would just give this to him—"

The receptionist made a sudden decision. "Hold on a minute. Let me buzz him." Before Tessa could protest, Ginny pressed the button on the intercom. "Chief, I'm sorry to disturb you, but Dr. McGuire is here. She says she has information for you. Do you want me to just take it or should I send her in?"

There was a slight pause, then Vince said, "I'll be right there."

Ginny gave Tessa a quizzical look as if wondering why the chief of police would come out to see her.

Tessa folded the index card to give herself something to do. She heard the door to Vince's office open and then there he was, striding toward her. He was wearing navy slacks and a white oxford shirt with a black bolo tie.

"This is a surprise. I thought after—" He stopped, realizing they had an interested audience.

"I have those names for you...physical therapists."

Vince knew as well as she did that she could have called. Just seeing him caused her heart to gallop at breakneck speed.

"Come on," he said. "I'll show you my office. You can tell me about the therapists."

If she left now, quickly, there'd be questions about why she'd come and why she hadn't accepted his invitation. But if she accepted his invitation, there would probably *still* be talk. Though her reason for being here *could* be pushed into the realm of a professional consultation. She was, after all, his son's doctor.

She nodded to Vince and started toward the wooden gate. He reached it before she did and held it open for her. When she passed him, she was very close to him—close enough to smell the scent of his cologne, close enough to stir up too many memories. By the time she reached his office door, she felt hot all over and told herself to calm down, to act as if Vince were any other classmate who'd moved back to Sagebrush.

Right.

Vince's office wasn't huge, but it was big enough to hold an expansive metal desk with a computer station to his right, four tall file cabinets and a set of barrister bookshelves. The yellow stucco walls were bare but a casement window provided a view of the back of the property. A stack of file folders toppled sideways on Vince's desk.

"I don't want to interrupt your work," she was quick to assure him. "I can see you're busy."

"I need a break." He gestured to the coffeepot on top of the bookshelves. "Cup of coffee?" Then he snapped his fingers. "You drink tea now. Sorry, I don't have any of that."

"I'm fine."

He looked over her, assessing everything from her striped tank top to her white jeans, then he motioned to the chair in front of his desk. She perched on the edge of the wooden captain's chair, fingering the index card she was still holding. "I have the names of two therapists. Both are good. You might be able to get in to see one before the other."

He came around the desk instead of sitting behind it, took the index card from her and sat on a corner.

At once Tessa realized he was much too close for comfort. Everything about Vince, from the jut of his jaw to his slim hips to his long legs reminded her of the times they'd spent together, riding, swimming, making love. She knew what was under his clothes and he knew what was under hers. Years had made his body harder and stronger. She could tell that by the way he moved, the way his muscles rippled. And *her* body? She was in shape, but she didn't know what he'd think of her now. After all, at thirty-eight, he was experienced. How many women had he been with since he'd been with her?

"Tessa?"

He must have asked her a question. "Sorry, my mind was wandering. What did you ask?"

"Are you sure you don't have a preference for which therapist is best?"

She shook her head. "Both treat babies."

He studied her. "Where did your mind wander?"

Heat crept up her cheeks. "I have to make rounds at the hospital later today."

"So you were thinking about a patient? Or were you thinking about us?"

She wasn't going to go there. "I know you're wondering why I came here today instead of calling. I guess…our time at the diner didn't go very well. I don't want to feel this awkwardness every time I see you. If we could just establish a friendly professional relationship—"

"Professional?" His eyebrows quirked up.

"Yes. I'm your son's doctor."

Vince's stormy gray gaze said he wasn't buying it. She could put whatever label she wanted to on their relationship, but it would always be deeper than whatever she described it as. That's what history did. It wound ties around two people that couldn't easily be severed.

Out of the blue he asked, "Are you seeing anyone now?"

She couldn't help her defensive reply. "That's really none of your business."

"Maybe not, but I thought I'd ask anyway. Are you?"

Was there a reason he was asking? A reason that had to do with those silver sparks in his eyes? "No."

"Then any awkwardness you're feeling isn't about that— about a boyfriend not liking the idea."

"No, it's not."

"So that means the awkwardness between us has to do with everything that happened, what we said and what we didn't say. We'll never resolve that over a cup of coffee or tea."

"Maybe we shouldn't try to resolve it," she admitted softly. "Maybe we should just realize we're different people now and go from there."

He leaned toward her. "Are we different people?"

Vince's cologne, the shadow of his beard on his jaw, the way he listened—as if she were the only one in the world to listen to—almost urged her to lean toward *him*. But then she concentrated on his question and wondered if Vince was thinking about her father and his involvement in their breakup, his involvement in her life. "Yes, we're different people. You're a father now and I'm the doctor I always wanted to be."

"Always?" he challenged.

For the span of her marriage, all she'd wanted to be was Vince's wife and the mother of his children. She'd told him that when they'd married. She might still become a mother if she was lucky—if someone chose her profile at the adoption agency…if an unwed mother picked her to adopt her child. But she didn't know what the possibility was of a woman choosing her over a married couple. There was no point going into her dream of adopting with Vince. It might never happen.

Studying his somber expression, knowing he was searching for answers as she had, she replied, "My dreams as a teenager had to change as an adult. Once I decided to become a doctor, that was my dream."

The quiet in the office became uncomfortable until she asked the question gnawing at her. Turnabout was fair play. "Are you dating? I mean, were you serious about someone when you became Sean's legal guardian?"

For a moment their gazes held but neither of them spoke. Then Vince answered her. "I wasn't seriously dating."

"I see."

He pushed himself up from the desk, all casual easiness gone. "No, you don't see, Tessa. I was a homicide detective— on call day, night and weekends. Unless I wanted to hook up with another detective who understood that—" He shook his head. "Most of those relationships don't make it, either. So when I dated, I dated for fun, to forget my work and have a good time. That's probably something you wouldn't under- stand because you were never that kind of woman."

"Is that a compliment or an insult?"

He blew out a breath in frustration. "Neither. You wanted a home and family, or you wanted a career. But whatever you wanted, you weren't the kind of woman who could have fun for a night and then forget about it."

"You were that kind of man?"

"I turned into that kind of man. But now that I have Sean to think about and focus on I have to be a role model and I have to be there for him 24/7."

She studied the set of his shoulders, the slide on his bolo tie in the shape of the state of Texas, which was a symbol of the professional responsibility he was shouldering. But the responsibility of fatherhood was even more daunting. "You seem to have accepted being a parent without much of a fight. Maybe it's what you wanted all along." Her heart hurt as she thought about the child they'd lost, a child Vince had been as excited about as she had been. She could see he was thinking about that little boy now.

"The past always surfaces, doesn't it?" he asked in a low voice.

"It's our common ground."

"Whether we want it to be or not." His gaze assessed her again from head to toe as if trying to figure out something. "Did you find the life you wanted?"

"I'm still working on it."

His jaw became more set, but then he said, "Good luck with that."

They were finished. They *really* were. There was too much hurt and resentment swirling under the surface.

What if they brought it all out into the open?

That might only make things worse.

Standing, putting a little distance between them, she motioned to the card on his desk. "I hope you like the therapists." She wouldn't see Vince again until after his consultation with Dr. Rafferty. If the specialist recommended surgery, then she wouldn't see Vince until after that surgery was completed. At that point, he'd probably be thinking about leaving Sagebrush.

"Good luck with Sean, Vince."

His expression was unreadable as he replied, "Thanks. I'll walk you out."

They obviously had nothing more to say. They obviously had too much to say and couldn't say any of it.

After he opened his office door, she was careful as she passed him that their bodies didn't touch. She was careful not to breathe in his cologne or glance back at him or remember. She pushed open the swinging wooden gate herself. He caught it and passed through after her.

At the glass door, she knew everyone in the room was watching them. She extended her hand irrationally, needing some kind of last contact.

He clasped it in both of his.

"See you around," she murmured.

"See you around." He released her hand.

As she left she felt as if she'd lost something precious she could never find again.

* * *

"One…two…three!" Vince chanted enthusiastically the following Monday as he raised Sean's arm up and down. After three, Vince put his lips to the little boy's tummy and blew a puff of air, making Sean giggle. Sean always giggled when Vince did that and Vince loved to hear it.

However, Sean stopped midgiggle and gave a little cough.

Vince studied his son then commented to Mrs. Zappa, who was folding laundry, "He's sniffling. I noticed it this morning when I gave him his bottle."

Mrs. Zappa was a short, robust woman, with rimless spectacles and gray salting her black hair. She was full of energy and seemed to love taking care of Sean.

Mrs. Zappa placed Sean's little shirts in a chest drawer and crossed to the changing table where Vince stood taking his son through the routine of exercises for his arm.

She studied the baby. "He ate this morning."

"Not as much as usual," Vince reminded her.

"Does he have a fever?"

Vince picked up the ear thermometer he'd bought. "According to this he doesn't, but maybe I'm using it wrong."

Mrs. Zappa took it from him and crooned to Sean. "Let me try to take your temperature, too." Afterward she scanned the readout. "Normal. But with a baby, that could change at any time. I'll check it every hour or so. We'll make it a game."

Vince glanced at his watch. "I should get going."

"Did *you* eat breakfast?"

A genuine homebody, Mrs. Zappa felt she had to mother him as well as Sean. He wasn't sure how he felt about that. It had been a long time since anyone cared whether he ate well or slept…not since he'd been married to Tessa.

"I'll grab something at the station."

"Oh sure, some of those pastries from the Yellow Rose. Don't you realize they're clogging your arteries?"

"I could just have black coffee," he joked.

Rolling her eyes, Mrs. Zappa picked up Sean, bouncing him in the air. The baby chortled and drew up his legs.

"Let me tell you something, Mr. Rossi."

He'd asked her to call him Vince, but she wouldn't.

"You might have lived your life just for yourself for a long time, but now you have the future to think about. You have to stay healthy for this little boy. He's going to need you around for many, many years to come. So in addition to working out with those weights in your bedroom, you need to eat right and take care of yourself."

She must have seen the weights when she cleaned and swept his room. "I hear there's a runners' path around the lake," he said. "I'd like to include that in my schedule a few times a week, but it might mean you'd have to stay another hour or so. How do you feel about that?"

"More money in my piggy bank for that cruise I want to take." She grinned at him and took Sean over to his crib, laid him down and started the wind-up mobile toy above him. The tiny animal figures moved around the circle in time with the music.

"I'm going to make chili for tonight. How hot do you like it?" she asked with a grin.

"Hot."

She shook her head. "Pretty soon I'll have all your tastes figured out."

Crossing to Sean's crib, Vince adjusted one of the figures on the mobile that had become tangled with another. When he gazed down at Sean, he held out his finger for his son to grasp. Sean grabbed it with his good hand and Vince hoped beyond hope that Dr. Rafferty could give back to the baby the use of his right arm.

Mrs. Zappa gazed at him across the crib. "You know what you need, don't you?"

He wiggled his finger back and forth with Sean holding on to it. "What? More cookware?" Mrs. Zappa had been dismayed when she'd arrived that he'd only bought a saucepan and a frying pan.

"Not cookware. You need a *wife*."

That brought Vince's gaze to hers. "I don't need a wife. I have *you*," he joked.

"Be serious, Mr. Rossi. I see you worry every time you look at that little boy. A wife would help cut that worry in half. A wife would help lighten the troubles and double the joys."

Before he thought better of it, he responded, "I tried that once and it didn't work out."

If that wasn't an understatement, he didn't know what was. He was sure Tessa still blamed him for everything that had happened, including her hysterectomy. He deserved the blame, the guilt and the regrets.

"I'm not husband material, Mrs. Zappa."

"Why do you say that?"

"Because my marriage failed. Because I never had a role model."

"You didn't have a dad?"

"I had a dad who drank."

"I see," she said slowly. "That doesn't mean you can't learn. If you want something bad enough, you do what you have to do. You learn what you have to learn."

As he thought about that, the end of his marriage played insistently in his head. Tessa had made her decision at the hospital when she chose to go home with her father rather than with him. Had he learned from *that?* He'd learned some bonds overrode others. He'd just been too smitten with Tessa to see it. "You make life sound so easy."

"Oh, no. Life isn't easy. Sometimes it's a downright struggle. But having the right person beside you makes all the difference in the world. My Tony…" She sighed. "He was the best husband in the world. He told me every day he loved me. He never hesitated to give me a hug or a squeeze. He was a good man who worked hard to make our life the best it could be. I'll never stop missing him. Thank goodness that, while I miss him, I have all the memories from thirty-six years of marriage to give me comfort. I can't imagine what my life would have been without him."

"You have children, right?"

"Two boys—one lives in Austin, the other in San Antonio. And because I have two boys, that's how I know you need a wife to help you raise your son."

Since his divorce, Vince never thought about committing to a life partner again. He simply couldn't imagine it. When he and Tessa had married, everything about the marriage had been strained from the get-go. She'd come from wealth and they'd had no money. She'd come from a ranch with every modern convenience. They'd had a walk-up apartment with very few amenities. She'd thought being married had meant spending time with him. He'd had to work from sunrise to sunset just to give them the basics, just to pay for doctors' appointments, the utilities, the repairs on his truck that was always breaking down. He'd had no expectations about marriage, but she had.

It was time to leave for work, but he had one more question for Mrs. Zappa. "So many marriages aren't good ones, so many fail. What was the secret to making yours a good one?"

The older woman saw he was serious and wanted an honest answer. Soberly, she replied, "There are *two* secrets—compromise and forgiveness. So many young people think love is enough. But it's not, not unless it grows into self-sacrifice, not unless both people can put the other one first."

As Vince left the apartment a few minutes later, his mind was on everything Mrs. Zappa had said as well as on every one of the mistakes he'd made when he was eighteen, naive enough to think that love *was* enough.

That evening Vince paced the kitchen with Sean in the crook of his arm. He did *not* want to call Tessa.

But Sean coughed once again, a cough that made Vince hurt for the little boy. Sean also sounded as if he was wheezing.

Making the decision that was best for his son, Vince went to the cordless phone, picked it up and dialed. Earlier he'd looked her number up in the phone book and he'd remembered it. If she didn't answer, if she wasn't home, he'd take Sean to the emergency room.

Tessa must have had caller ID because when she picked up the phone, she asked, "Vince?"

"I'm sorry to bother you, but Sean's sick. He just had the sniffles this morning, but now he has this cough and a temperature of 101 and he's wheezing. He's done the emergency room route before when his parents died and he was in the hospital, too. I want to spare him that if I can."

After only a moment's hesitation, Tessa said, "Give me your address."

He quickly did, telling her what side roads to take off of the main street.

"I'll be there in ten minutes," she assured him and cut off the call.

Until Tessa arrived, Vince paced, rubbed Sean's back and laid him in his crib. When the coughing seemed worse, he picked him up again. Ten minutes seemed like an hour, but Tessa finally rang the doorbell.

He hurried to answer it, Sean in his arms.

Tessa was carrying her doctor's bag, and although she wore jeans and a short-sleeved blouse, she had a professional air about her. After one look at Vince's face, she took Sean from him and carried the baby to the sofa.

Vince felt absolutely helpless and hated the feeling.

Now Sean was crying, as well as sniffling and coughing. Tessa tried to soothe him as she examined him. When she listened to his chest with a stethoscope, she frowned. "You said this has been going on since this morning?"

"Yes. It was just a cold."

"It's more than that now. I want you to run the shower, hot water. Get a lot of steam in the room. After you do that, find me a bath towel to wrap him in. I'm going to give him an injection and then sit in the bathroom with him until he's breathing better."

Vince came over to Sean, laid his hand on his son's head. "Maybe I should stay here with him while you give him the injection."

Tessa gazed up at him. "The sooner you get the shower running, the sooner he'll breathe easier. Trust me, Vince."

He realized he *could* trust Tessa, the doctor. And Tessa, the woman? She'd chosen her father's protection over his but that didn't matter right now. Only Sean mattered.

As he left the living room, he glanced back at Tessa. She was reaching into her bag, taking out a vial of medication.

He hadn't prayed in a very long time. But he prayed now that Sean could fight this off and soon be well.

Chapter Four

Tessa sat on the closed commode in Vince's bathroom, cooing to Sean and rocking him. Her hair was soft, fuzzy and damp from the steam, tendrils curling this way and that. Her clothes were damp, too.

Vince didn't think she'd ever looked more beautiful.

His own shirt was sticking to his skin but he'd been so worried about Sean that he hardly noticed. The baby had stopped coughing and his wheezing didn't sound as constricted.

"We can't keep him in here much longer. I'll run out of hot water. What then?"

"I don't think we'll need a trip to the emergency room. Can you go to the drugstore and buy a cool mist humidifier and distilled water? Also, Pedialyte. I want him to drink it so he doesn't get dehydrated."

Vince glanced at his watch. It was after nine but he knew the drugstore was open until midnight.

"Oh, and children's acetaminophen if you don't have any."

"Are you going to stay in here until I get back?"

"If your hot water holds out," she said with a small smile.

He was so tempted to wrap his arms around her and Sean, to tell her how grateful he was for her expertise, for coming when he knew she didn't want to be here.

Instead, he said, "Thank you, Tessa."

Her gaze locked onto his for a few seconds—a few seconds of awareness and memories and sizzling attraction that was still there.

But then she looked away and gazed down at Sean. "No thanks necessary."

Her voice was a bit unsteady.

As Vince climbed into his SUV, he couldn't keep from envisioning how Tessa had massaged Sean's little chest and patted him softly on the back when she'd first taken him into the bathroom. She was so good with children.

And she'd never have any of her own.

Vince knew Walter McGuire had blamed him for everything that had happened, from the pregnancy to the quick marriage to the walk-up apartment he and Tessa had lived in, to the condition that had taken their baby and almost Tessa's life, too. Over the years, Vince had wrestled with his own guilt and attempted to look over that span of time rationally, especially the pain that had come from Tessa choosing to go home with her father from the hospital, rather than with him. Everything that had come after had been born in that decision of hers. And whether he wanted to admit it or not, the pain from her choice still lodged in his heart.

He found what he needed in the drugstore and was home in twenty-five minutes. *Home.* It wasn't home yet. Maybe it just needed pictures on the walls in the living room and a few rugs on the floor? That might help. But how long would he and Sean be staying here? If Sean had surgery, how long would recovery take?

Next week he might have that answer.

Now when Vince stepped into his house, something felt… different. Maybe it was the lingering scent of strawberries and vanilla from Tessa's lotion or whatever she used. That day she'd come to the station, it had wrapped around him and twisted his gut. Or maybe the difference in the condo came from the sight of her medical bag sitting on his dinette table.

But then he was drawn to what really transformed his condo into a home rather than simply the place where he lived. The sound of Tessa's lovely voice crooning to his son pierced his heart.

He never should have called her tonight. Yet Sean had needed her. What else could he have done?

His training in the Air Force and as a cop had taught him to walk silently unless he wanted to be heard. Setting his purchases quietly to the side of the computer on his desk in the corner of living room, he went down the hall to Sean's room and stopped just outside the doorway. Tessa's hair and blouse were still damp. She'd tossed a towel over the back of the rocker and had wrapped Sean in one.

Vince could see his son was sleeping as Tessa rocked and sang, "Baby close your eyes. Dream of puppy dogs and fire-flies."

He didn't know the song and wondered if she'd made it up herself to sing to her little patients.

He knew he hadn't made a sound. He'd hardly taken a breath. Yet she glanced up and spotted him as if some sixth sense had told her he was there.

"Is he asleep?" Vince asked though he'd already guessed the answer.

"Yes, he's breathing easier. The little guy was tuckered out. He drank some apple juice for me. If he wakes up later, he might be sweated. See if he'll take some of the Pedialyte."

"Let me get the humidifier going and we'll see if he'll sleep in his crib."

After Vince added the distilled water to the machine and plugged it in, Tessa asked, "Do you have something easy we can put on him so we don't wake him?"

From the chest of drawers, Vince produced a nightshirt that buttoned down the front and was decorated with baseballs and bats. Tessa carefully unwrapped the towel. Vince slipped one little arm into the sleeve and carefully snuck it around Sean's shoulders. When he did, the back of his hand grazed Tessa's breast. She gave a quick inhale of air. They both froze.

He mumbled, "Sorry," and managed to slip Sean's good arm into the sleeve without awakening him. Vince's big fingers fumbled on the snap buttons.

"Would you like me to fasten them?" Tessa asked softly.

He nodded, too close to her to shove his desire aside. He noticed Tessa's fingers tremble as she fastened the bottom three snaps.

Lifting Sean from her arms, Vince wasn't thinking about the past and regrets as he settled his son in his crib. The electricity between him and Tessa was alive now and it caught him in its grip. He turned on the night-light, then adjusted the baby monitor to the proper volume.

Tessa came over to stand beside him as he looked down at Sean. "He's a wonderful little boy."

Vince thought he heard a catch in her voice. "I should

make a tape of that song you were singing for nights when I have trouble getting him to sleep."

"It's just something I made up for when I visit the newborns in the nursery."

"You're a woman of many talents."

She smiled. "Believe me, songwriting isn't one of them."

He wouldn't agree but didn't argue with her. Standing so close to her, he could sense when she shivered. "You really should get out of that blouse. Let me get one of my shirts and I can run yours through the dryer."

Tessa was never uncertain, but she looked unsure now. "I really should be going."

"Mrs. Zappa made freshly squeezed orange juice this morning with the juicer. Can I tempt you?" The housekeeper at Arrowhead Ranch used to give Tessa freshly squeezed orange juice every morning.

"You remembered." Tessa's blue eyes were wider with surprise.

"I remember a lot of things."

He could have kissed her then. He could have just bent right down and slid his arms around her. That's what everything inside him urged him to do. But a kiss right now could damage the fragile thread of understanding forming between them.

After a last glance at Sean, Vince went to his room to find a clean shirt. Fortunately, Mrs. Zappa had ironed a few yesterday.

Away from Tessa, he inhaled a deep breath and took a white oxford, one of many he had because they were so practical, from his closet and carried it back to Sean's bedroom where she was still watching his baby.

When she took the shirt, he said, "I'll be in the kitchen pouring orange juice."

He closed Sean's bedroom door behind him, giving her the privacy to change…the privacy to think about their lives intersecting again.

A few minutes later, Tessa walked into the kitchen, feeling self-conscious in Vince's shirt and knowing she shouldn't. But when they'd been married, she'd sometimes worn one of his shirts with nothing underneath it and that had often led to—

She banished thoughts of their past together. Making sure she'd buttoned Vince's shirt up to the neck, she told herself once more that there was nothing to be self-conscious about. Still, when Vince's gaze slowly scanned her, she felt naked. She felt foolish; color crept into her cheeks.

She went to the counter where he had taken a pitcher from the refrigerator. "This housekeeper of yours must be a gem if she squeezes fresh orange juice for you."

"She is. Already I don't know what I'd do without her. I think she's trying to mother me, though, and I don't know how I feel about that."

Tessa had never known her mother and in some ways, she believed her loss was easier than Vince's situation where he'd had a mother one day and the next day he hadn't. "You could let her do nice things for you. There's nothing wrong with having parents who care, even at our age."

As soon as she said it, she knew her words were a mistake.

Vince's brow creased and he handed her one of the glasses he'd filled.

She took a few sips, not knowing where to take the conversation from there. Her father was definitely a hundred-pound gorilla standing between them in the room.

She grasped for an easy topic. "So how do you like being chief of police?"

He shrugged. "It's okay. I'm pushing around a lot of papers, though. I'm used to being in the thick of things."

"Fortunately, we don't have much murder and mayhem in Sagebrush."

"Fortunately," he agreed.

That change of subject hadn't done so well.

The kitchen was furnished as sparsely as the rest of the house. There was a dining area with a table and chairs but it looked as if it was never used. There were no curtains or blinds, no place mats, not even a pad and pencil that said Vince spent some time here. But there was a calendar hanging by a magnet on the refrigerator. She noticed the appointment she'd had with Vince and the one with Dr. Rafferty were marked. Then there was a notation about his meeting at the high school. The rest of the blocks were empty.

She realized Vince hadn't begun his life here yet.

"I know what you're thinking," he said gruffly.

"You're a mentalist now?" Although her tone was teasing, she remembered all those times years ago when he could read her mind and she could read his. From the moment they'd first spoken to each other, they'd been so in sync.

He didn't banter back. "You're thinking a child should be raised in a real home, not just in a condo that's a place to stay."

He definitely wasn't reading her mind tonight. "No, that's not what I was thinking, Vince. I was thinking you've just begun a life here. It will take some time to establish it…if you want to."

After he studied her thoughtfully, he admitted, "I couldn't see putting money into rugs and drapes when we might only be here a few months. Except for Sean's room. I wanted his room to be a special place for him."

Setting her glass on the counter, she asked, "So you really intend to leave again?"

He set his glass down, too, and stuffed his hands into his pockets. "When I found the specialist in Lubbock, I thought coming back here would be a good idea. Since I was familiar with the area, I was able to get in touch with a couple of friends. I believed Sagebrush would be good for Sean because we wouldn't be landing in a strange place. But as soon as I drove down Longhorn Way, I thought 'strange' might have been better. I have very few happy memories here, Tessa."

She knew that was true—a mother who'd abandoned him, a father who hadn't known how to be a father. Vince had had to be the parent. He'd had to pay the bills and work after-school jobs to keep food on the table. Then when he'd married her, he'd had double the responsibility.

When Vince slipped one hand from his pocket, Tessa knew what he was going to do. She should have grabbed her medical bag and fled. She should have…but she didn't.

He reached out and brushed her hair from her cheek. His rough skin on hers was as arousing as it always had been. Even back in high school, his hands had been callused from outside work. Trembling, she couldn't look away from him, couldn't step back, couldn't forget what they'd once been to each other.

"Your perfume suits you." His voice was husky and there was a fire in his eyes that meant he desired her. She could never forget that heat or hunger.

"You shouldn't…" She couldn't seem to get out any more words.

"I shouldn't what? Touch you? We've been avoiding each other like we had the plague. I don't think that has to do with lack of chemistry, but too much of it. It's still there. Even worried about Sean, I want to feel your skin under my hand."

He could always do this with words—make her need. He

straightened the collar of his shirt around her neck and under her hair as if that were the most natural thing to do. But then his hand slid along her collarbone, his fingers lacing in still-damp strands of her hair.

When Vince's lips brushed over hers, her breath caught, her heart raced, her stomach twittered. Before she realized what she was doing, she reached for him, too. Her body was reacting as if it knew what was best.

He murmured something against her lips, something like, "I don't believe this is happening."

But then she heard nothing but the hum of the refrigerator and concentrated on the sensation of Vince's lips on hers. He had always been an expert kisser, even at eighteen. Now, there was no finesse about the kiss, no intentional seduction. She felt his deep hunger, felt hers rise up to meet it, welcomed the invasion and sweep of his tongue in her mouth, the press of his body against hers. Old and new, familiar and different, excitement and desire mixed with the thought that what they were doing was taboo…yet she couldn't remember why.

Suddenly, a baby's sharp cry penetrated her pleasure. Instinctively her body shut down. She broke the kiss, and Vince pulled back.

He said gruffly, "I have to check on him."

Of course he did, and she wanted to run into the room with him. Already she cared about this child as she did all her patients. But she stayed put as if she were glued to the spot.

Mechanically she picked up her glass, drank more orange juice and didn't think about the kiss, didn't revel in the lingering sensations from it, didn't wonder why she'd let it happen.

When Vince returned, she was still standing there, counting the tiles along the back of the sink.

"He's okay," Vince told her. "He must have cried out in his sleep. Sometimes I wonder if he has dreams about the accident, if he'll subconsciously remember that forever. Or if he's so young, it will be wiped away as if it didn't happen."

Almost as if she had no control over her thoughts or her voice, she faced Vince. "Why didn't you contact me after you went away?"

He didn't seem surprised that she'd slipped back twenty years. His brows furrowed, the nerve in the hollow of his jaw worked and he replied, "You'd gone on with your life. I didn't want to interfere with that."

"How did you know I'd gone on with my life?"

"I still had friends back in Sagebrush. My dad was still here. You know how it is."

She knew how it was and should have realized he'd gotten word of her comings and goings, just as she'd gotten word of his.

He stepped closer to her and rested his hands on her shoulders, sending heat through her once more. "I also didn't want to put more of a wedge between you and your dad. I saw what it did to you when he disowned you, when he told you that you were no daughter of his. When I left, you were back in his house, back in his life. What would he have done if I'd contacted you?"

"He didn't have to know," she replied defiantly. If Vince had asked her to join him *anywhere,* she would have forgotten about college to build a life with him.

But Vince shook his head. "You never could have kept it from him. I saw how you needed your dad after the hysterectomy."

His words tore her in two because he still didn't understand. "I didn't only need my dad, Vince. I needed *you,* too.

I lost our baby and you weren't there to talk about it. You weren't there to…understand."

Suddenly Vince's house was claustrophobic. She couldn't be in the same space he was. She couldn't breathe. Pulling away from him, she went to the table and grabbed her bag.

"I'll mail your shirt back to you," she murmured and hurried to the door.

She practically ran to her car parked at the curb. She didn't look back at the house to see if he'd followed her outside.

He wouldn't follow her. He wouldn't leave Sean. That's the way it should be.

When she started the ignition and drove away, a mantra played in her mind. *You can't fall in love with him again. You can't fall in love with him again.*

On Saturday morning, Tessa slid a tea bag into a mug of hot water and absently dipped it up and down. All week she'd tried to forget about her kiss with Vince on Monday. When she concentrated on her little patients, she could pretend nothing had happened with him. But it had. She hadn't wanted to dissect the kiss. Yet she couldn't set it aside, lock it in a box or think around it.

Francesca, dressed in jeans and oversize T-shirt with the Family Tree symbol stamped on the front, sank onto a stool at the eat-in counter of their kitchen, looking as if she'd been up all night. Her long hair was tousled, and she wore no makeup. *That* was unusual. Francesca was a perfectionist about almost everything and her appearance was out of character.

"Are you okay?" Tessa asked, picking up her mug and carrying it to the table.

Francesca considered her question. "I don't know."

"Do you want to talk about it?"

Instead of answering, Francesca slid from the stool and went to the coffee Emily had brewed before she left to go grocery shopping. She poured a mug and worried her lower lip.

"What happened?" Tessa prompted.

Her friend took a sip of coffee and grimaced. "No wonder Emily adds milk and sugar. This is strong enough for two pots."

Turning on the faucet, she added hot water, then crossed to the stool and took a seat once more. "I went to a party last night."

"That's right!" Tessa remembered. "It was a reception for Kent Harris to celebrate the opening of his own law firm in Sagebrush. Do you think he snagged many clients?" If she could encourage Francesca to talk, maybe Tessa could discover what was troubling her friend.

"Possibly. There were so many people there that—" She stopped abruptly.

"What?"

Francesca stared down into her coffee.

Worried now, Tessa laid a hand on her housemate's arm. "What's troubling you so? Was Darren there and he wants to get back together with you again?"

The reason Francesca had moved to Sagebrush was to be with a man she'd fallen in love with. Darren was also a doctor at Family Tree. He'd met Francesca at a conference, and they'd conducted a long-distance relationship until he'd persuaded her to move to Sagebrush. She had and, for a while, their romance had stayed on an even keel. But when Francesca had moved in with Darren, she'd discovered he wasn't the man she'd thought he was. He'd taken her moving in as a commitment, the next thing to marriage, and he'd seemed to change before her eyes into the type of controlling man she'd sworn she'd never date, let alone marry.

"Nothing to do with Darren," Francesca answered her, but then frowned. "Or…maybe it does in a roundabout way."

She ran her hand through her straight hair and sighed. "Why is it that just when I think I've learned from my past, that I've finally broken free from the kind of abusive home I grew up in, something happens that tosses me right back there again? Before I could talk, I knew my mother was under my dad's thumb. When I was little, I learned why when I overheard Mom confiding in a friend, telling her my dad had forced her into marriage when she'd gotten pregnant. After Darren turned out to be controlling just like my dad, I swore off relationships."

"I know you did. In the year since you've broken up with him, you haven't even gone out on a date."

"Yeah, well, I slept with a man last night. How is that for jumping into the fire?"

Tessa saw the panicked, troubled look in Francesca's eyes. "You used protection?"

"Oh, yes, he had a condom." Francesca sighed again and rubbed her face, then she shook her head. "Honest to goodness, Tessa, I don't know what happened."

"You mean he put something in your drink, or—"

"Heavens no."

Tessa thought it was best if Francesca started from the beginning. "Who is this man?"

"Your dad probably knew *his* dad. In fact, you might even know him. His name is Grady Fitzgerald. His father was a saddlemaker and now Grady's taken over the business."

"Sure, I know him. Vince probably knows him, too. He worked in his dad's saddle shop when we were married, though Grady was away at school then. My dad bought my first saddle from Mr. Fitzgerald and Grady delivered it to the ranch."

"What was Grady like?"

"From what I remember, he wasn't a joiner. Lots of girls had a crush on him but he seemed immune. He comes from a big family. He was a good rider and that's probably why he's so good at saddle making. He understands what the horse and rider need to be comfortable."

Since Francesca was listening with avid interest, Tessa asked, "Are you going to see him again?"

She shook her head adamantly. "No."

"Why not?"

"Because we're very different people. We talked for a long time, Tessa, and I realized *how* different we were while we were talking."

"Different how?"

"My career and the babies I treat mean everything to me. You know that. I'm on call more often than not, and I'd *never* say no when a baby's in distress. It's my life. Grady's business is just a *part* of his life. He spends a lot of time with his family. Family has never done anything but hurt me…from my father's abuse to my mom's fear. I always felt I had to take care of my mom because she couldn't take care of herself."

Soon after Francesca and Tessa had become friends, she'd learned her story. Francesca had revealed that her mother had finally left her husband after he'd attacked Francesca when she was eight. But the years of being in the house with him, under the same roof, knowing he could control her mother because she was afraid of him, had scarred Francesca deeply. Her mother had died a few years ago from lung cancer and Francesca had once confided she felt like an orphan.

Now Tessa reassured her friend, "You have us. Me and Emily. You know you can count on us."

"I know I can. But that's different from what Grady has. He's used to being part of a bigger picture. I'm used to being on my own. And it's not just that. Grady's about seven years older than me…in his midforties. He wants to stay in Sagebrush the rest of his life. You know I'm thinking about applying to Doctors Without Borders and seeing more of the world."

Tessa let silence settle in for a few seconds. "So what's the real reason you don't want to see Grady again, in spite of all these differences?"

After a long moment, Francesca replied, "Exactly because I *knew* we were very different and something *still* happened. I was so attracted to him that differences didn't matter and all we had was this…heat!" Francesca shook her head. "Besides, I'm not ready for a relationship. It hasn't been that long since Darren."

"It's been a year."

"It doesn't seem like very long, and let's face it, Tessa. I don't trust men—not with my history with my dad and then not with Darren turning into somebody I didn't know. He was so charming before I moved in with him, then he became controlling and manipulative and everything I didn't want in a man."

"You made a mistake."

"Yeah, a big one. Apparently I was attracted to what I was trying to run away from. I can't take the chance that that's going to happen again."

Tessa knew all about being afraid of making the same mistake twice.

The doorbell rang and Francesca's eyebrows raised. "Are you expecting someone?"

"No, how about you?"

Francesca shook her head.

Before Tessa went to answer the door, she suggested, "Maybe it's Grady."

That comment drew Francesca through the living room into the foyer after her. But when Tessa opened the door, she didn't find Grady Fitzgerald. She found Vince with Sean in his arms and a bag in his hand. She couldn't have been more surprised.

Obviously seeing that, he explained, "We had our physical therapy with Carly Brennan this morning. She could fit us in first. It went really well. I just wanted to return your blouse and tell you how grateful I was for your recommendation." He handed her the bag.

She'd mailed Vince's shirt back to him the morning after their kiss. With Francesca almost hovering over her shoulder out of curiosity, Tessa said, "Why don't you come in. Vince, this is one of my housemates, Francesca Talbot. Francesca, Vince Rossi." The two shook hands as Tessa smiled at Sean, who seemed to be in robust health again. "How are *you* this morning? So you liked Carly, huh?"

Sean waved his left arm, tried to sit up against Vince's chest and talked the baby syllables he knew best.

"He's adorable," Francesca cooed, always interested in babies. "Will he come to me?"

"He might," Vince said. "He's not shy of strangers."

Tessa wanted to hold Sean, too, play with his little fingers and toes, brush his wisps of hair. But she knew she had to keep her distance. She couldn't become involved with this baby any more than his father.

Francesca held out her hands to Sean and he went to her without any fuss. "I'll take him out back to the yard. There's a lot to look at out there."

Sean seemed content with Francesca and didn't even look back at his dad as she carried him away.

"She's good with kids," Vince observed, watching Francesca as she talked to Sean and he happily babbled back.

"She's a neonatologist. She fills her life with helping newborns." Then remembering ingrained manners, Tessa asked, "Coffee?"

"I had two cups while I was waiting for Sean. I think that's enough for now."

Tessa motioned to the sofa and Vince lowered himself to it. After setting the bag with her blouse on the end table, she sank down beside him, then realized she shouldn't have. Their elbows were almost brushing. She turned sideways a bit but then her knee grazed his. Neither of them moved away. "Did Carly let you stay for the session?"

"Some of it. She spent a long while just making sure Sean was comfortable with her."

"I understand that's what she's good at. She needs her patient's cooperation and she usually gets it."

Silence fell between them and when Tessa glanced at Vince, she felt all twittery inside.

"You look as if you're going to jump up and fly away," he remarked in a dry tone.

She made herself consciously relax and settle back into the sofa cushion. There was about a half inch of space between them and she was thankful for that, at least. She couldn't move farther away without seeming too obvious.

"I feel like a teenager again," he muttered, stepping into the void between them.

"Why?"

"I don't know what to say or do with you, Tessa. At least when we were teenagers, I didn't get the feeling you'd rather be anywhere else than sitting next to me."

"That's not the case," she admitted, then wished she hadn't.

His eyes darkened with memories and, gazing at him, she felt the old sizzle, the old pulsing awareness, yet something new, too. Still, she protested, "We're not teenagers anymore. We're old enough to know what's right for us and what isn't, what's good for our lives and what isn't."

"Maybe we're fighting too hard *not* to remember, fighting too hard *not* to regret. We can't deny what we had, what happened. Don't you think we can get past it? I can't live in a vacuum while I'm here, Tessa. And Sean needs people around him who care about him."

"Maybe I don't want to care about Sean," she confided. "Maybe it hurts too much."

"Tessa," he said gently, reaching out and touching her face, just like he used to when he was trying to comfort or console her. Her instinct was to back away, yet her heart was telling her not to move.

Could they move beyond the past?

"I came over to do more than thank you." Vince dropped his hand. "Remember I said I was in touch with Ryder Greystone?"

"Yes, you said he's on the Lubbock P.D."

"He's having a party tonight and invited me. He told me I could bring a guest. Would you like to go?"

Could she become friends with Vince? Could she get to the point where being together with him again was natural, not awkward? If he was going to be around town, she probably would see him and after all, Sean was her patient. But going to a party with him?

"Would this be a date?" she asked cautiously.

He tossed her a wry smile. "It would be whatever you want it to be."

"Can I think about it and call you in a couple of hours?"

She saw his frown. "Unless you're going to ask someone else if I say no."

"No. I'm not going to ask anyone else. A couple of hours will be fine." After a look at her that told her better than words he was thinking about kissing her, he stood. "I'd better get Sean and take him home for lunch."

As Vince turned to head toward the kitchen, Tessa clasped his forearm. "I don't want to jump into anything I'll regret."

"I understand, Tessa, believe me I do. But it's just a party. We're simply going as friends. There doesn't have to be more to it than that."

Maybe that was true for Vince, but it wasn't true for her. If she went to this party, she'd be saying "yes" to letting him back into her life. Would that be a foolish decision or a mature one?

She needed a few hours to figure it out.

Chapter Five

Beside Vince, at the door to Ryder Greystone's house, Tessa wondered if she'd made a mistake by accepting his invitation. Vince had the rough appeal of a tough guy, always in control of himself in any situation. Yet the seductive appeal for her had always been his gentle hands and his tender heart. He only let that show, however, when he knew it was safe to do so. He was showing that side of himself with Sean and that's what made him so hard to resist.

Ryder's door suddenly flew open and the tall, good-looking cop stood there grinning at them both. "Well, well! Like old times. I told Vince to bring a guest but I never guessed it would be *you*."

She and Vince had been awkward with each other in the car because this felt too much like a date. It didn't help that he looked incredibly sexy in a black V-neck T-shirt and chinos. She didn't need Ryder's words to remind her what they'd been. "Not old times," Tessa replied agreeably. "Just two friends running into each other and catching up."

Vince tossed a quick glance her way at her explanation and took off his Stetson. "We both need some R & R and thought we could get it here."

As if Ryder was suddenly aware of the tension between the two of them, he stepped back and motioned them inside. "There's plenty to eat and lots of folks to mingle with."

Vince offered his friend the box of imported chocolates he was carrying. "You can add this to the buffet."

"Great. There aren't any more classmates here, but, Tessa, you probably know a few of these people because they bring their kids to you." He addressed Vince. "Some of the guys are here from the station, so you'll have plenty to talk about. There's music on the patio in case anybody wants to dance."

Tessa was surprised by how many people were crowded into the small house.

Vince must have been thinking the same thing because he said, "You could get lost in here."

A bit of the tension seemed to ebb between them.

"I haven't stepped into a room where I didn't know anybody for a long time," she admitted.

"Not a partygoer?"

"Hardly. You know me, Vince. I focus on what's in my life and don't see much around it."

"*Do* I know you, Tessa?" His gaze was penetrating, trying to see into corners where she didn't want him to see.

The phrase had just slipped from her mouth and she chastised herself for not monitoring her words more carefully. "Some things about me haven't changed," she said honestly. "How about you?"

"The party scene was never my gig, but as far as walking into a room where I don't know anybody, that happens a lot."

"Investigating homicides?"

"Yeah."

His brief answer told her that he didn't want to talk about his years as a detective.

Then he looked thoughtful for a moment. "You have to deal with strangers all the time, don't you?"

"You mean dealing with new patients? The funny thing is, they never seem like strangers. Focusing on their child gives us a bond."

"You were always all about bonds."

His voice was neutral and she couldn't tell what he meant by that. "Is that a bad thing?"

"No. I was never like that until I met you."

They'd both grown up without mothers but under different circumstances. Tessa had always missed her mother, even though she'd never known her. Her mom was like a piece that had been lost from her heart, and Tessa could never find it. That's why she and her dad had stayed so close. But when Vince had lost his mother, apparently he and his dad had emotionally gone separate ways. She didn't know if Vince had ever connected with anyone and held on for dear life. When they were teenagers, she'd thought they were holding on to each other.

But he'd let go.

A woman waved at Tessa from across the crowded room and she was grateful for the distraction.

"You know her?" Vince asked.

"She's a medical secretary for one of the internists at Family Tree. Do you mind if I head on over?"

"Of course not. I'm going to rub elbows with some of the guys in the Lubbock P.D."

As Tessa headed for the secretary, Vince went in the opposite direction. She breathed a sigh of relief. Being close to Vince put her on guard, kept her on her toes, urged her to protect her heart. Making small talk would be a wonderful break from that.

For the next two hours, as one conversation led to another, Tessa didn't see Vince much, though she was aware of him at the far corner of the room talking with three men, then in a serious conversation with Ryder in the kitchen, and later loading his plate with a burrito and enchiladas. It was as if she had "Vince-radar" and couldn't turn it off even if she wanted to.

The living room grew warmer in spite of the open windows and the screened sliding doors leading outside. Her wrap-around, silky, blue blouse felt almost molded to her back. She smoothed her hands over the thighs of her new jeans and excused herself from the conversation on the sofa. She needed fresh air. The colored lights drew her to the patio where the music had wandered from oldies to a salsa beat to everything in between.

As soon as she stepped onto the patio, she spotted Vince seated casually in a lawn chair, a tall bottle of water in one hand. Where most of the guys were drinking beer, he wasn't. She wondered if he ever did and if not, was it because of his job? Or because of his father?

She was enjoying herself at the party, but coming with Vince? It was like she was with him, yet she wasn't.

Purposely heading in the opposite direction from him, she stopped at the ice chest and was trying to decide if she wanted a soda or water when a hand clasped her shoulder. It was Vince's. Years had gone by but not so many that she couldn't remember what the touch of his hand felt like.

She turned, not knowing what to expect.

"Care to dance?" Vince asked in that casual way he had of making the important seem unimportant. There were couples all over the patio, some dancing, some sitting quietly in lawn chairs talking. The music had turned slow and dreamy and although the patio was covered with an awning, the black sky beyond was studded with stars.

"We're at a party, Tessa. Dancing's just part of it. No big deal."

Right, it was no big deal to be held in Vince's arms.

She walked into his hold and, for a few moments, silence pulsed with attraction they couldn't deny was there. Unnerved by it, she said, "I guess you have a lot in common with the men here tonight."

"Yes, I do."

"You said you and Sean's dad were friends as well as partners?"

"We were. We had each other's backs. He was like a brother and when he married Carol, she was like family, too. She *was* family. I spent more time at their place than my own. And when Sean was born—I'd just come off a shift and was waiting at the hospital with Scott. I got to see Sean shortly after Scott did. He came out and got me."

Tessa could hear the huskiness of emotion in Vince's voice, and she realized how deeply he'd cared about his friends and about the baby who'd become his son.

"So Sean has no other family?"

"Only his great-aunt. I'm not sure what to think about her. I have to take pictures of him this week and send them to her. I suppose it's better to stay in touch than not."

Vince went quiet as they swayed to the music, in unison stepping to the left, to the right, front and back, his strong body intimately guiding hers. She shouldn't let the intimacy happen. She closed her eyes, feeling burdened by the past, uncertain in the present.

His hold tightened and she opened her eyes. They'd come to the edge of the patio. Glimmers of light streaked the border of the flagstone.

Vince urged, "Come with me for a minute. I want to ask you something."

He held her around the waist as they stepped off the patio onto the gravel and he tugged her around the side of the house. The moon was three-quarters full and her heart pounded with excitement. What could Vince want to ask her?

He stood close, as close as they'd been when they were dancing. "What do you feel when you see me with Sean?"

That wasn't what she expected, though she didn't know what she'd assumed Vince would ask. Did he think that pulling her into the shadows would help her give him a more honest answer?

"Vince, we shouldn't leave the party. Everyone's going to wonder—"

"No one's going to miss us and you know it. There are too many people here for anyone to notice. Answer me, Tessa. What do you feel when you see me with Sean?"

She didn't want to look at Vince, she really didn't. She'd blocked thinking about how she felt with very good reason. Now with his question, she couldn't block the emotion anymore. She could picture Vince bringing Sean into her office the first time, how she'd noticed right away how comfortable the baby was in his arms, the tender expression on Vince's face. The night he'd called her to his condo, he'd been so worried. Before he'd put Sean to bed, the baby had nestled into his shoulder, knowing safety. And when he'd brought Sean to the house—

Her chest tightened and her throat almost closed, but not altogether. She managed to say, "It hurts, Vince. It hurts so much. I see our baby, *our* son, and I just ache."

The tears came so fast she didn't have the opportunity to blink them away. They rolled down her cheeks and caught on her chin.

Then Vince was holding her, his hand on the back of her head. He was stroking her hair, his lips at her temple.

"I'm sorry," he murmured. "I'm so sorry."

Her breath hitched, and she couldn't remember the last time she'd let herself cry like this.

One hand still on the back of her hair, Vince leaned away slightly and raised her chin with his thumb. A car door slammed.

The chatter of the party was just around the corner. The music smoothed into something bluesy and Vince's mouth came down on hers. She was seventeen again, and he was everything she'd always wanted. The sweep of his tongue was possessive, and she kissed him back as if time and fate and distance hadn't kept them apart.

Then as suddenly as she was overcome by his kiss, she rejected it. She rejected *him* and tore away.

"No! No, this *isn't* happening. This can't happen. I won't let it. You're here now, but you're going to be leaving again. I have a life here, a life I want. I'm going to—"

She'd almost told him she was going to adopt a child, a child who needed her and a home just like Sean needed him. But she couldn't confide her most important dream to him, not when she'd just confided her deepest hurt. She did not want this closeness or need it. She'd only be hurt by it. She knew that because she'd been hurt by him once before.

She tried to turn and run, but he held her by her shoulders.

"Stay still, Tessa. Stay still. I'm not going to hurt you. I'm not going to do anything. I never should have started this here, but I knew you didn't want to be alone anywhere with me. I knew you'd never let me start this conversation if I didn't spring it on you now."

"And what good did it do, Vince? So now you know I hurt every time I see you with Sean. What good is that?"

"It's honest."

She inhaled slowly and then let her breath fade out of her mouth. "I'm going to go home. I can get a ride with someone."

"Don't be ridiculous. I'll drive you. I've had enough party to last me a while."

They both had. Maybe tomorrow she could put this in perspective, but right now she couldn't.

Sitting with Vince in his SUV, Tessa was grateful when his cell phone rang. The silence between them practically rippled in its intensity, but she knew nothing either of them could say would break it.

"Rossi," he barked into his phone after he put it to his ear.

Tessa listened as he asked tersely, "When did it happen?" A pause. "Where?" Another pause. "I'm on my way, ETA ten minutes." He glanced at Tessa as he put his flashers on and sped up. "There's been an accident over on Route 82. Teenagers. I've got to get there. I can have an officer take you home."

"Don't worry about that. I might be able to do something to help."

"Emergency services was called. The paramedics were dispatched. They'll probably be there when we get there. But if you can help, too, I'm sure everyone will be grateful."

"How many kids?"

"Six, from the eyewitness account. Let's hope it's not more."

She knew better than to ask any questions about the accident. Until they were on the scene, nothing was for sure. Her stint in emergency medicine had not been one of her favorite rotations. She'd treated sullen gang members from drive-by shootings, knife wounds, heart attacks, strokes, and a multitude of other injuries and ailments. What she'd disliked most about the E.R. service was that there never had been any follow-up, not by her. If possible, patients were dispatched to their family doctor's care. Many didn't return to the E.R. The ones who did saw whichever doctor was scheduled for that day. Now Tessa looked forward to follow-ups, to the resolution of patient care.

"Are you often called out?" She knew Vince had a lot of administrative work to handle.

"If something major happens. If other jurisdictions are involved. I have to make sure protocol is observed and everything's done by the book."

"Mrs. Zappa will watch Sean for you without any notice?"

"Without any notice."

Five minutes later they drove up to the scene. Red, blue and white flashing lights practically illuminated the sky. Both cars from the accident were smoking, twisted pieces of metal. They looked older, possibly with no air bags, probably fix-up cars like Vince's truck had been.

She and Vince both jumped out of his SUV. He headed toward one of his officers. Tessa aimed straight for the paramedic in charge. She usually carried her medical bag wherever she went but tonight she didn't have it. Tonight she'd wanted to forget she was a doctor and just be a woman.

But she should have known that wasn't possible.

While she spoke to the medical responders, one ambulance pulled away, sirens blaring.

"We're waiting for two more ambulances," the EMT told her. "Two kids in the back of one car and one in the other weren't wearing seat belts. We're transporting them first."

"Where do you need me?" she asked.

He motioned to two teenagers stretched out on the ground, blankets covering them, and IV lines already running. "Check on them and make sure vitals are stable. The girl has a broken leg. The guy's shoulder is dislocated. Then you might want to check on the three kids talking to the police. They said they were okay but after an accident like this, we'll want to examine them anyway."

After inspecting the injured teenagers where an EMT monitored them, Tessa made her way toward the berm away from where the firemen were dealing with the crash vehicles. Three more teenagers were huddled there, blankets around them, while Vince and one of his officers spoke with them.

She asked Vince, "Are you finished with any of them?"

"Start with Linda," he suggested gently, gesturing to the blond teenager to the right of the other two.

She crouched down beside Linda and asked quietly, "Are you dizzy? Short of breath? Anything like that?"

Linda shook her head.

Tessa asked her to scoot down a few feet from the others so she could take her pulse and her blood pressure with the cuff she'd lifted from the paramedic's van.

"I'm worried about Amy," Linda said, her voice catching. "Is she going to be all right? They took her away in an ambulance. After the crash, she wouldn't answer me when I called to her."

"Once we transport your friends to the hospital, we'll know better how they're doing. Now I just want to make sure you don't have to go there, too."

The wail of sirens was almost earsplitting. Two more ambulances pulled into the crash site and screeched to a halt. Tessa knew scenes like this were parents' worst nightmares. She just hoped everyone here would be returned to their family safe and sound.

Tessa stayed at the scene long after the ambulances had pulled away. Someone handed her a cup of hot coffee and she sipped at it to stave off the slight chill. She'd heard bits and pieces from officers' conversations as well as emergency personnel. The kids in one car had been drinking. They had run a red light and slammed into the other car. She wouldn't want to be doing what Vince was doing now, making calls to the kids' parents.

Then he was on the move again, striding toward her fast.

"I have to get to the hospital and talk to the parents of the kids who were most seriously injured. John will take you home."

"I'll go with you."

"Why?"

"Because I know the parents of the girl who was most seriously injured, Amy Garwin. I treat her younger brother and sister. I might be able to help somehow."

The wide brim of Vince's hat shadowed his face. She couldn't really see into his eyes.

"All right," he finally agreed, "but I have to ask some tough questions. Don't get in the way of that."

"I won't."

After a studying moment, he nodded, and they hurried to his SUV.

* * *

At the hospital, Vince questioned the two teenagers who were injured but conscious and spoke with their parents. He was aware of Tessa at first consulting with medical personnel, then conversing quietly with Amy Garwin's parents. The mom was crying and her husband's arm circled her.

Vince's stomach clenched and his chest grew tight. When he'd inquired about Amy's condition, the nurse had told him the teenager was not conscious and tests were being run. He didn't want to intrude on her parents at a time like this, but he had to talk to everyone at some point. That's just the way it was.

Tessa was seated in a chair across from the couple. He introduced himself, then consulted his notepad.

"You're Mr. and Mrs. Garwin?"

The couple nodded, the petite redhead holding on to the arm of her husband.

"Do you have to do this now?" Tessa asked in a low voice.

"I'm afraid I do. How is your daughter?" he asked Mrs. Garwin.

Her eyes brimmed with tears. "She's not waking up. They can't make her wake up."

"They're doing an MRI," Mr. Garwin explained. "That's why we're waiting here."

Respecting what they were going through, Vince kept his interview short. After all, Amy hadn't been driving. She'd been one of the passengers in the backseat of the tan sedan, not wearing her seat belt.

When he finished with the Garwins, he consulted with a paramedic who had first arrived on the scene. Tessa and the couple disappeared.

Vince sank into one of the chairs to review his notes, to

make sure he hadn't left anything out or forgotten details. The insurance companies were going to have a field day over this one and he wanted to make sure every *i* was dotted and every *t* crossed. Besides, it kept him from thinking of the teenager who wasn't waking up, the girl who would be having her leg set, the boy with the dislocated shoulder. One carful of kids had been doing what they were supposed to do, driving home after a pool party with friends. The other carload of kids had been drinking. He wanted to slam his fist through a wall, just like he'd wanted to do some of those nights when he'd come home and found his dad drunk on the living room floor. But he'd learned long ago to channel his anger into something more productive.

He stood when he saw Tessa walking toward him. It was hard to believe mere hours ago he'd been holding her in his arms. She'd felt good there…too damn good. Was that why he'd messed up the evening with his question? What had he intended to accomplish by making her voice the pain they'd both experienced?

"Are you finished here?" she asked, glancing at his notebook.

"For now. I can drop you off on the way back to my office. I want to do the paperwork while it's still all fresh in my mind."

"You go ahead. I'm going to stay here for a while with the Garwins."

"What did the tests show?"

"Amy has a severe concussion. Now we just have to wait and hope."

Vince's grip tightened on the notebook. "I can't imagine being in their position. Elective surgery with Sean is bad enough."

"Amy was in the car with the kids who weren't drinking. If she'd only had her seat belt on—"

Vince shook his head. "You can tell them what to do and teach them right, and still this kind of thing can happen. Why would anyone want to be a parent?"

"You tell me," Tessa suggested softly.

"I'm sorry, Tessa. I shouldn't be talking about this with you."

She brushed her hair over her shoulder and gave a shrug. "I have to face these kinds of conversations a lot with the parents of the kids I treat. I manage to detach most of the time. I understand what you're saying, Vince, but *you* already know the other side of it. You know the deep joy of having Sean grip your finger, of holding him in your arms, of seeing him smile. There's no way to prevent the heartache. You can only hope the joy outweighs it."

He was reminded again of how strong a woman Tessa had become. She wasn't the teenager who had looked to her father for support and comfort. "How are you going to get home?"

"I know many people here. There's a nurse up on Amy's floor whose shift ends in a couple of hours. She'll give me a ride back to Sagebrush."

"And if something happens and you decide to stay the night?"

"Then Francesca or Emily will come and get me. Don't worry about me, Vince. I'll be fine."

In other words, she didn't need him. He'd take her at her word.

She glanced over her shoulder at the elevator. "I'd better get back up there. Thanks for inviting me to the party tonight. I don't socialize as much as I should."

"We're going to talk about what happened."

She shook her head. "There's no need to talk about it."

Her voice was sure of her conclusion, yet in her eyes he saw a flicker of uncertainty. No matter what she thought, they had something to finish.

"Sean's appointment with Rafferty is this week. I'll let you know if we're going ahead with the surgery." He slid the pen he'd been using into his pocket. "Take care of yourself, Tessa."

"I will," she murmured.

He turned and walked away first. But as he exited the hospital, leaving didn't feel right…just as leaving hadn't felt right twenty years ago.

Chapter Six

On Friday afternoon, Tessa was between patients at her office when the receptionist peeked around the inner door. "You received a call from Vince Rossi. He asked if you'd phone him at your earliest convenience."

Tessa knew Vince wouldn't call without a good reason. He would just leave a message on her home phone if he wanted to…invite her to another party? Talk? Try to finish something that would never have an end?

No, if Vince was calling her here, he had word on Sean.

Taking out her cell phone, she slipped into her office and shut the door. His number was one of the few on her call list. She hit Send and waited.

He picked up on the second ring. Without preamble, he said, "Dr. Rafferty believes surgery will give Sean full use of his arm."

"That's wonderful! How soon does he want to do the surgery?"

"Next Tuesday—early."

Vince didn't sound overjoyed or relieved, and she guessed why. At his continued silence, she asked, "Vince?"

"He's only seven and a half months old, Tessa. The idea of anesthesia scares me as much as the possibility that surgery might not go well."

She understood his concerns, but she also knew Vince needed to stay as optimistic as possible for Sean's sake. "Don't borrow trouble. Dr. Rafferty's one of the best. You've got to be positive about this and not let Sean feel your fear."

He was quiet for a moment, then asked, "And just how am I supposed to keep from worrying?"

She knew Vince would never admit he was afraid. "You can worry, just don't let it show. Think about Sean catching a baseball, throwing a pass, lifting a fork with his right hand. See those pictures in your mind and don't let go of them."

"Is that how you get through the tough times? You imagine good outcomes?"

"As often as I can."

"You would have made a good cheerleader," Vince joked.

"I wanted to try out, but…" She stopped, not delving into that territory.

"But your dad wouldn't let you because of the short skirts?" Vince guessed.

"Something like that. I think he was more afraid I'd climb to the top of one of those pyramids and then break something. You can't let your concerns hold Sean back."

"I know that. Right now I'm trying to decide whether or not I should tell his great-aunt that the surgery is scheduled. I could just wait until it's all over."

"Wouldn't *you* want to know?"

"I'm not sure. I can save her worry if I call her after the fact to tell her it was successful."

"On the other hand…"

"On the other hand, Janet is his only living relative. She deserves to know what's happening with him," he admitted to himself and to her.

Caring about both Vince and Sean in spite of the warnings she'd given herself, Tessa offered, "Would you like me to come to the hospital Tuesday morning? I have office hours in the afternoon and evening."

"Only if you want to."

Want to. Need to.

Tessa wasn't sure what was going on with her and Vince, what was in the past and what was in the present. But from her experience as a pediatrician, she knew how parents felt when their children went to surgery. They usually had family support. Vince and Sean were alone.

"I'll find you after rounds."

"I'll understand if you get tied up, Tessa."

When she closed her phone, she knew she was getting involved again. She couldn't help herself. But she'd make sure her defenses were firmly in place. She'd make sure she kept her heart safe.

Vince was determined to stay by his son's side while the nurses prepared him for surgery. For the most part, they let him. He touched Sean often—a hand on top of his head, fingers stroking his baby arm, his expression as calm and serene as he could make it for his son. For a while, he had no idea that Tessa was standing in the doorway watching him, but when he looked up, there she was.

She was all business today, in green linen slacks, a cream

blouse, with a white lab coat over it all. A little of his attention slipped from Sean to her. She made his heart jump, damn it.

Tessa crossed the room and stood beside Vince, smiling at the nurse who was putting a little paper cap on Sean's head.

"They have to take him now," she murmured to Vince, meeting his eyes.

Had Tessa known how very difficult this moment would be? Vince wrapped his fingers around Sean's little hand. Tessa must have understood his sudden panic because her expression was full of empathy.

"Trust Dr. Rafferty," she encouraged him.

"This isn't just about putting my trust in a surgeon," Vince returned in a low voice. "It's about Sean being separated from me, the one anchor he's got in this world right now. It's about any pain he might experience. If I could go through this instead of him, don't you think I would?"

As his gaze held Tessa's, so many emotions rushed through him. Even though they'd been teenagers at the time, they'd known each other as intimately as a man and woman could. That intimate knowing was still there whether or not either of them wanted to admit it.

Tessa succumbed to it as she stepped closer and clasped his arm. "You have to see the outcome in your mind. You have to believe Sean will handle surgery easily, heal quickly and have use of his arm for years to come. Concentrate on *that*, not on the rest."

When she released his arm, Vince wondered if he'd deluded himself about a bond between them. Tessa must have given this same speech to countless parents. "This is old hat for you, isn't it?"

A shadow of vulnerability passed over her face. "Never.

Believe me, Vince. Seeing one of my patients go into surgery is never easy and it never 'doesn't matter.'"

"You'll burn out, caring so much," he predicted, again pushing away pictures of the shy seventeen-year-old she'd once been.

"You mean I'll burn out if I don't stop caring, so I should detach myself and walk away? I can never be that kind of doctor. For me to help people, compassion is as important as skill. And I'm not so different from Francesca and any other doctors who work at Family Tree and in this hospital."

The nurse, also wearing a paper cap and scrubs, said to Vince, "I have to take him now."

Vince knew this wasn't life-and-death surgery, but he also knew anything could go wrong. He concentrated on the picture of Sean throwing a baseball, touched his son's cheek, whispered to him, "I love you. I'll see you soon," and then stepped back from the gurney.

Tessa gently touched Sean's cheek.

As the nurse pushed the gurney down the hall, Vince balled his hands into fists and all of his control held him back from running after the stretcher.

Tessa touched him lightly on the shoulder. "Come on. Let's get some coffee."

Vince focused on her, thinking coffee was the last thing he needed. His stomach was burning with worry.

Then she made another suggestion.

"Or we could go to the chapel."

"I was in a church for Scott and Carol's funeral. That was the first time since I was a kid. My next-door neighbor had taken me when I was around eleven."

"It's a place to find peace and comfort," she offered in a quiet voice that wasn't coaxing but rather sure.

"Do you still go to church?" She had when they were teenagers.

"Yes, I do. Every Sunday. The same church I was christened in."

How had they ever gotten together with their different backgrounds, with their opposite lifestyles? "All right," he agreed. "We can try the chapel, but I doubt if I'll worry any less while we're there."

Ten minutes later, they were seated in the pews and Vince didn't know what he was supposed to do. He glanced at Tessa and saw she had folded her hands in her lap and her eyes were closed.

If he closed his eyes and inhaled deeply, maybe he could relax…if nothing else. He tried it but without much success.

Tessa must have sensed his restlessness. "Do you ever just go outside at night and look up at the sky and feel the…immensity of everything?" she asked softly.

He knew what she was getting at. "I think that's why I stayed in Albuquerque. The sky there—during the day *and* at night—just seems to lift you up. The cliffs and the mountains even more. Sometimes I'd just stop by the side of the road, get out of the car and stand there in the sun looking into the sky, or into…I don't know, something much bigger than me."

"Can you think about that now? Can you think about the best for Sean *and* you?"

"Are you saying that's praying?"

"Yes, I think it is."

Their shoulders were touching, and so were their hips and thighs. But at the moment, he wasn't revved up because he desired Tessa. He was revved up because this closeness, this talking about something as intimate as prayer seemed so right. Tessa amazed him. There was always a deeper place he could go with her, where he could always find what he needed.

He did as she suggested and, in a while, realized his breathing had slowed. Hope for Sean's future drove the fear from him.

After a while, they both sat back and he covered her hand with his. "Thanks for being here."

She gazed at him but said nothing. He knew that was best. They were just here in the moment and that's the way it had to be.

Dr. Rafferty was somber as he stepped into the waiting room later Tuesday morning after Sean's surgery.

Vince stood immediately, Tessa close beside him. He was grateful she'd gotten him through this three-and-a-half-hour waiting time by talking about Sean, pulling stories from Vince about his stint in the Air Force, relating how she and Francesca and Emily had met and lived in a house together. She'd kept conversation rolling to keep him from thinking.

Now, with her elbow brushing his arm, he felt Sean had two champions no matter what happened.

The surgeon strode to Vince and nodded. "The nerve reconstruction surgery went well. I also removed scar tissue that had been blocking nerve signals. I believe Sean will be one of the fortunate ones, if you're willing to be patient."

"I can be patient," Vince assured the doctor with rough emotion in his voice.

"What *will* be the recuperation time?" Tessa asked.

"His arm will be in a soft sling for about three weeks. Then he can start physical therapy. But we won't see results for four to six months and it could be years until he has full use of his arm."

"Can we see him?" Vince asked, needing to know his son was really okay.

"You'll be able to see him in recovery in about a half hour. After he's alert and his vitals are good, we'll settle him in a room."

A short time later they were standing by Sean's crib. Tessa crouched down on one side and murmured to the little boy. Sean responded with a smile and a babble.

"What did you tell him?" Vince asked.

"That he's the best little boy in the whole world."

Vince crouched down at his son's other side and Sean turned his face to his dad. "We're just going to treat this like a great adventure. You won't be alone from now on, cowboy. I'm staying here with you tonight. We'll be together until you come home."

Vince couldn't tell if Sean understood or not, but his son reached for Vince's hand.

Tessa stood gazing at both of them. "I'm glad you're staying tonight. Sean will feel safe and protected…and loved."

"I hope so. Sometimes it's easier to know the right thing to do than at other times."

Tessa's and Vince's gazes locked.

The beeping of the automatic blood pressure monitor interrupted the sweep of memories that always seemed to suck them in.

The sound gave Tessa the opportunity to turn away and check her watch. "I'd better go. If I start office hours on time, I might finish at a decent time. When I get finished, would you like me to bring you takeout?"

"That would be great. I probably won't want to leave him."

"I can imagine what you're feeling, Vince, but when Sean naps, take a break. You need to take care of yourself, too."

He was staring at her over his son's crib, thinking about

the two of them together…the two of them taking care of Sean together. Was that too crazy to hope for?

"Do you care if I take care of myself, Tessa? Do you care about Sean's outcome as more than his doctor?"

They were in a corner of the recovery room with medical personnel stationed at the other end.

"Vince, this isn't the place—"

"Isn't it?"

Her eyes were wide with a vulnerability she rarely showed him.

"I care about you *and* Sean. Maybe too much."

Tessa believed those were the words he needed to hear right now. Her denial had ended because they *were* true. Maybe after this crisis, they could figure out how involved they were going to be in each other's lives.

Tessa peeked into Sean's hospital room at nine o'clock that night, gripping two take-out bags. Vince had pulled a chair over to the crib and laid his hand on his son's arm. The tableau touched Tessa deeply and she gripped the bags a little tighter. Just what had she admitted to Vince this afternoon? What had he deduced from it?

She entered the baby's room now and spotted the recliner that had been rolled in so Vince could stay the night. He was unaware of her presence until she tapped him on the shoulder.

He went still for a moment, then rose from the chair. "I'm losing my instincts," he said gruffly. "I should have sensed you coming."

"All of your attention is on Sean. I can understand why you didn't."

He shook his head. "That's no excuse." He inhaled deeply and smiled at the bags in her hand. "Is that food?"

She grinned back. "I don't know what's going to happen if you eat enchiladas this time of night, but I know they're your favorite. At least they used to be. You haven't sworn off of them, have you?"

He laughed. "No."

Handing Vince the bags, she went to the crib and looked down at the baby. "Has he been awake?"

"On and off. He fell back to sleep a little while ago. He's been through a lot. I'm just grateful Rafferty thinks the surgery was successful."

"Remember, the improvement will happen slowly."

"I know. I'll be patient about it. I have no choice."

Tessa was close to Vince and she liked the sensation of her shoulder bumping his. Vince had always made her feel safe and protected and cared for. Until—

Until he'd been silent and uncommunicative when he'd visited her in the hospital. Until he hadn't objected to her going home with her father.

She couldn't help but lean over Sean and whisper in his little ear, "I hope you're having sweet dreams, baby. You deserve good dreams from here on out."

Tessa could feel Vince's gaze on her and she swallowed hard. Turning toward him, she said, "I'm sorry I'm so late. I had an emergency and then patients got backed up."

"You don't have to apologize, Tessa. You don't even have to be here." He raked his hand through his hair. "Sorry, that didn't come out the way it should have. I just mean...I cornered you in the recovery room today. I'm surprised you came back."

She admitted she cared about him, but she wasn't going to tell him she couldn't keep away. "Come on, let's eat. There's a taco salad there for me."

With a vinyl chair pulled near the recliner, they ate in the dimly lit room, the hospital noises outside the door seeming far away. A nurse came in to check on Sean and then departed once more.

After Vince had downed the enchiladas and half of his soda, he said, "I'll probably take Sean home late afternoon tomorrow. In the morning, the physical therapist is going to show me exercises for his wrist and thumb and fingers. It will be a few weeks before we can do anything with his shoulder."

"Are you nervous about taking him home?"

"Not nervous. Just concerned he'll need something and I won't understand what it is."

"Would you like me to come over tomorrow evening? I could just check and make sure everything's okay."

Vince studied her for a long time.

"What?"

"I'm going to owe you a few Texas T-bone dinners or a room full of flowers when this is all done."

"You don't owe me anything."

Again he was silent for a few moments, then he asked, "Will you answer a question for me?"

"Maybe. It depends on the question."

He shook his head and chuckled. "I should have known." Then he sobered. "You said you care about me and Sean. Is that why you're here?"

"Does it matter? I help friends, Vince, and they help me. That's the way small towns work. You know that."

"Maybe I'd forgotten, or maybe I just never experienced small-town life the way you have. When my dad was passed out on the living room floor, I don't remember anybody helping."

She imagined him as a young boy, in a situation much too

complicated for him to figure out on his own. "Did you ever ask for help?"

"Hell no! It was a matter of pride for both me and Dad."

"So why are you accepting *my* help now?"

His expression changed, going from serious to much lighter. "Because you have great taste in restaurants," he joked, pointing to the crumpled bags on the floor beside his chair.

"Vince."

With a sigh, he ran his hand through his already disheveled hair. "I knew you wouldn't let that pass," he grumbled. Finally he admitted, "I'm not sure. Probably because you care about Sean. You care about babies and you know what you're doing. Since you're a doctor, Sean needs you to watch out for him. I'll never deprive him of that, pride or no pride. I guess I'm learning that by being a parent, I can't let anything stand in the way of what's best for him."

She knew that was the right answer, but maybe she'd wanted a different answer. Maybe she'd wanted him to say that he still felt connected to her on some level. Maybe she'd wanted him to admit that whatever was between them so many years ago wasn't yet finished. Heck, she'd just admitted that to herself after their last kiss. She hadn't wanted to consider it before. Denial was a great wall that could keep worries and complications at bay. The problem was—it was a wall that always crumbled.

Right now she was tired, not just physically tired, but emotionally drained. She'd worried along with Vince this morning and she knew she was becoming entirely too invested in Sean's welfare, not to mention Vince's life. But that would soon end. Sean would be recuperating and then Vince would be leaving. So if she wanted to play Good Samaritan or friend, there was no harm in that.

She *wasn't* involved with Vince.

Her salad only half-eaten, she settled the lid on it and stuffed it into the bag.

"That wasn't much of a supper," he scolded.

"It was enough. I've got to get going or Francesca and Emily will send out the search dogs."

"They don't know where you are?"

"Not exactly. I just told them I wouldn't be home until late."

After Vince pushed himself up from the recliner, he took his empty bag and dumped it in the trash can. "Are you taking that home to finish it?"

When she shook her head, he took the bag from her and tossed it into the can on top of his.

"If you had your choice, which would you pick? Flowers or the steak dinner?" he joked.

She rolled her eyes.

"Humor me."

Would she choose the safety of flowers, or the complication of a dinner with Vince? That's what he was really asking, wasn't it?

"I like flowers," she decided, taking the safe route.

"That's good to know." His gaze was trying to turn her inside out. Before it did, she moved toward the door.

She stopped before exiting the room. "You can call my office tomorrow and let me know when you're home. I'll be there until after five."

"Will do."

The light was too dim to read his expression.

As she murmured, "I'll see you tomorrow," and left the room, she heard him call, "Drive safely."

She had taken safe roads up to this point in her life. Were safe roads really what she wanted?

That was a question better left unanswered for now. That was a question that was better left unanswered until after Vince left Sagebrush.

When Tessa arrived at Vince's condo around seven o'clock, Mrs. Zappa was still fussing in the kitchen. The housekeeper had opened the door to Tessa and exclaimed, "Maybe you can make him eat!"

Tessa wasn't sure if Mrs. Zappa was talking about Vince or Sean. In fact, she'd never been introduced to the housekeeper and wondered how Mrs. Zappa knew who she was. "I don't think we've met," she began.

"Oh, I know who you are. You're Walter McGuire's daughter and you were once married to Vince." Conspiratorially, she leaned toward Tessa. "I've never told him I know, but I do."

Tessa had to smile in spite of herself. "Do you think he'd be uncomfortable if he knew you knew?"

"You know men. They like to keep their life private. If he wants to do that, it's fine with me. I'm not going to poke where I'm not wanted. He only let go of that boy to get a shower since he brought him home from the hospital, and now he's holding him again. Vince needs to take care of himself, too. The casserole's still in the oven. It's going to be dry as toast if he doesn't eat it soon."

"I'll see what I can do," Tessa assured her. "How is Sean?"

"From what I can tell, that little boy is doing fine. He ate *his* supper."

Tessa laughed. "That *is* a good sign."

Mrs. Zappa moved toward the door. "It was good to meet you, Dr. McGuire."

"It was good to meet you, too, but please call me Tessa."

"And you can call me Rhonda." She gave a last wave and left.

Moments later, Tessa was standing outside Sean's room. A small CD player on top of the chest played soothing music. Vince was sitting in the rocking chair with Sean asleep in his arms. He was looking down at his son as if he never wanted to look away.

"How's he doing?" she asked softly.

Vince gently touched the sling on Sean's arm. "As long as I talk to him and play with him, he's not fussy. I guess it distracts him from any discomfort he's having."

"Rhonda says you need to eat your supper. Now would be a good time if Sean's asleep, don't you think?"

"Rhonda?"

"Mrs. Zappa. She told me I could call her Rhonda."

He frowned. "Yeah, that was the name on her application. I've just never used it." Standing with Sean in his arms, he carried him over to the crib and gently laid him down. "I hate to leave him. I don't want him to wake up and be afraid, or think he's still in the hospital."

"You'll hear him on the baby monitor if he cries. You've got to give yourself a breather, Vince. Have you even slept in the past two days?"

"I got a few hours' sleep the night before surgery, and again last night."

"In a recliner in Sean's room."

"It was comfortable."

"Has anyone ever told you your stubborn determination can be frustrating?"

He smiled at her. "I've always considered it one of my better traits."

When he smiled like that, she felt butterflies flutter in almost every part of her body. She was *only* here to help him with Sean. "I haven't had supper, either. We can share Rhonda's casserole."

Tessa decided to serve their meal on the coffee table in the living room because Vince needed to relax. Maybe he would if the atmosphere was casual enough.

When he came into the living room and saw the two steaming plates, he admitted, "I think I *am* hungry. I had a sandwich from the cafeteria but that was a long time ago."

"This looks great."

Vince sat beside Tessa and dug his fork into the casserole.

They ate in silence for a few minutes until Tessa asked, "Are you going to work tomorrow?"

"I'm going in late. That way I can make sure everything's okay with Sean and Mrs. Zappa—Rhonda—before I leave. I'll stay late if I call home and everything's okay."

"You're not going to call her every hour, are you?"

He gave Tessa a sideways glance. "How did you guess?" Then he smiled. "No, I'm not going to call every hour. I trust her. The doctor said the incision on Sean's shoulder and the one on his leg looked good. I changed the dressings and Sean didn't seem to mind too much."

Tessa knew the surgeon had removed nerves from Sean's leg to replace damaged nerves in his shoulder. "It doesn't sound as if you really need my help."

He shrugged. "It's nice to have someone to eat with, but you don't have to stay if you have things to do."

"Nothing important." She had medical journals waiting but she had to admit she'd much rather be here with Vince. That was dangerous. Whenever she reached toward the coffee table, her arm brushed his. His knee was terribly close to hers. She could breathe in the scent of fresh aftershave, and she noticed his jaw was clean-shaven.

"I stopped in to see Amy during rounds again today."

Vince put his empty plate on the coffee table and set his fork on it. "I've been keeping updated on her, too. No change, right?"

"No change. Her parents and sister take turns talking to her, playing music, almost constantly. The doctors say that stimulation can't hurt. No one knows for sure if coma patients can hear all of it on some level, or if it helps bring them back. Some neurologists believe it does."

"If I were in their shoes, I'd try everything, too."

"I know what you mean."

Suddenly, they weren't eating anymore. They weren't staring straight ahead. They were gazing into each other's eyes.

Vince shifted toward her, bringing them into closer proximity. She didn't move away.

"Tell me something, Tessa, did you come here tonight simply because of Sean?"

Nothing about her situation with Vince was simple, not even her concern about his son. "I came…" She hesitated as she tried to be honest about her motive. "I came because I thought Sean might need me, and because you might need me."

"Do you care if I need you?"

She wasn't ready to go deeper, not ready to look at what might happen between the two of them if she let it. "What ways would you need me, Vince? That's the thing."

"There's one very basic way."

The desire in his eyes had nothing to do with his son, or even with their past. It was a hunger that was present, here and now, for her. If she were honest with herself and with him, she'd have to admit to the same hunger. It had increased in intensity since his visit to her office. She'd tried to push it down. She'd tried to turn it away. She'd tried to deny it existed. But whenever she was with Vince, it was there.

When he leaned even closer, she felt almost dizzy. He

stopped about an inch from her mouth. It was as if he was waiting for her to pull away. She briefly thought about it, but by then his mouth had covered hers, his tongue was teasing her lips. Afterward, he nibbled at the corner, then made the kiss serious.

Vince's sensual side had always swept her away and tonight was no exception. His lips and tongue explored her, delved deeper, fueled a response from her she'd forgotten she was capable of. As her fingers laced in his hair, his arm went around her. She felt enfolded in a fantasy, and her body came alive. Every sensation was exciting and new. She let go of the restraint she usually held on to tightly. She released the womanly need she barely recognized. She banished the past and the future and only thought about now. Vince always had that effect on her. He instilled in her a sense of passion, made her feel new and different, exciting and so alive.

It was the most natural thing in the world when his large hand slipped from her shoulder, passed over her collarbone and settled on her breast. His thumb trailed around the outline of her bra until he made smaller circles. Finally he targeted her nipple. She restlessly shifted her hands from his hair, down his back, until she could grab handfuls of his shirt. She pulled it up and out of his jeans, as eager as he was to feel more. He continued their kiss through their fumbling for buttons. Finally she had his shirt open and her hands were on his chest hair, sifting through it, dipping lower, reveling in his hot skin against her palm. His groan was deep and urged her to keep going. She unfastened the snap on his fly.

Vince had never taken her pleasure for granted, and now he didn't just enjoy what she was doing to him, but made sure she was feeling the fire, too. He easily unhooked her bra and slid his fingers under the material, making her crazy with a teasing, tantalizing touch of fingertips. This man had always undone her. He had always shown her new roads to passion. He'd always—

Always?

There was no *always* with Vince. There was no forever. How could she have forgotten that for even a moment? She never wanted to experience the pain of his leaving as she'd experienced last time. She'd lost their baby and was grieving and he'd just left…left without looking back.

She pulled away from his lips, his hand, his body so close to hers and was shaking her head before he could even ask any questions. "I can't do this. It's a mistake. We can't become intimate again."

Vince settled his hands on his thighs, swivelled away from her and took a few moments to compose himself. Then he asked gruffly, "Tell me something, Tessa. Do you believe it was a mistake for us to have *ever* become intimate?"

She knew what he was asking. They'd been so different, their worlds so far apart. Yet they'd connected in a way she'd never connected with another person. "I think back then, we had a chance. But fate intervened and we didn't handle it well. Now I make sure whatever fate dishes out, I control my own destiny."

"That sounds real good, Tessa, but what does it mean?" There was an edge to his voice as he turned to look at her now.

"It means that because you left once, I can never believe that you won't walk away again. That's why I can't get involved with you."

She could see the startled realization on his face when he understood what she was saying.

His gray eyes were dark, filled with past memories. "I never meant to hurt you." He paused and studied her still-flushed face. "I need to know something. Would you have given up becoming a doctor to be married to me? To live in a dump and be alone most of the time while I worked just to put food on the table?"

He was doubting her level of commitment back then and she couldn't blame him. "I'm not idealistic enough to believe love conquers all, but when I was seventeen, I believed what we had was enough. You're the one who left and jumped into another relationship. How could you have done that so soon? It sent me a clear message that I hadn't meant as much to you as you'd meant to me!"

"*You* filed for divorce."

Yes, she had. Because her father had told her that was best, because she'd felt alone, because she'd believed Vince had left her behind.

More upset than she wanted to be, much too close to tears, Tessa fastened her bra and buttoned her blouse. "Rehashing the past isn't going to get us anywhere, Vince. I should have known better than to…to…"

"Care?" he filled in. "Have you walled yourself off completely from your needs? Have you blamed me for everything that happened in the past without looking at your part in it? Have you decided never to risk having a serious relationship again?"

"A serious relationship only works when both people are serious. It only works if they're in the same place. It only works if they commit their lives to each other and *mean* it." She rose to her feet. "I'd better go."

But Vince stood, too, and caught her arm. "Don't run from what's happening between us, Tessa."

"Are you going to *stay* in Sagebrush?" she asked.

"I don't know yet what's going to happen. A lot depends on my position as chief of police and Sean's recovery."

"My home is here. My practice is here. My dad is here."

"And you won't uproot your life for a chance at something better." He made it a statement rather than a question.

"I've learned to cherish what I have, appreciate it and not expect too much." Her voice shook as she finished and pulled away from him.

He didn't try to convince her to stay. He let her go as he had so many years ago.

Chapter Seven

"So why did you go to the party with Rossi?" Walter McGuire asked Tessa. He sat in a nubby recliner in his den, rubbing liniment on his shoulder.

"That isn't what you use on the horses, is it?" she asked to lighten the tension a bit. She'd told him Vince was back and why. The fact that he already knew she'd gone to a party with the chief of police also told her he'd already known everything she'd just revealed.

"I might as well get the stuff I use on them and use it on *me.* It's a heck of a lot cheaper than this special formula that doesn't help a bit."

"Special formula?"

"Some herbal company over in San Antonio made it up for me. Don't change the subject. I'm not too old to notice."

Her father was sixty-seven now, almost bald except for a fringe of gray circling his head. He was as active as he could be with his arthritis. "I wasn't trying to change the subject. I needed time to think about the fact that you already knew Vince was in town. Why didn't you just say so?"

He stopped rubbing and looked at her. "I wanted to hear you tell it, so I'd know what you were thinking."

"And what am I thinking?"

"You're feeling sorry for him and his boy. You're already getting in too deep. I can tell by the way you say their names."

"I'm not in too deep and I do *not* feel sorry for anyone. Vince is a great dad. You should see him with Sean." She tried but couldn't keep the defensiveness from her voice.

"That's exactly what I mean. You can't even talk about it without getting all mushy inside. I know you, Tessa."

"So you know me, and I know you, better than we did twenty years ago. Any decisions I make this time will be without your influence."

He sighed, soothing his shoulder and arm with his hand. "So you don't want to hear what I have to say?"

"You can say whatever you want, but that doesn't mean I'm going to listen to your advice."

He blew out a breath and put the lid on the jar. "Sometimes you are the most frustrating female."

"I'm glad it's only sometimes," she teased.

After he pulled his shirt around him, he stuck his arm into the sleeve. "I didn't think you'd stop in tonight after rounds."

"Francesca and Emily went to a movie. I stopped in to sit for a while with that teenager who was in the accident. I just felt restless when I was done, so I came over here. Are you ready to turn in?"

"No." He motioned to his feet. "I didn't even pull off my boots yet."

"I ran into Tim Daltry when I was speaking at the high school one evening. He said you gave his son a job."

"Tim's been my bookkeeper for as long as I can remember. He always does good work. His son's a hardworking kid and he deserves a good education. I'm just helping him along a little." Her dad rose, went over to his desk and picked up a pamphlet there. He brought it over to her and set it in her lap.

"What's this?" It was a brochure about the Bureau of Land Management's adopt-a-horse program.

"I've been doing some reading. The government's thinning herds and they've no place for the horses to go. George Baldwin adopted one of them."

George was a rancher her dad knew from a neighboring county.

"And?" she prompted.

"And he said they're sturdy critters and wonderfully made. Their Spanish heritage shows. He e-mailed a picture of a mare. She's a beauty. The thing is if these horses aren't sold by the third auction—" He stopped. "You don't want to know. So I thought maybe we could take a drive the day of the auction in August and bring one or two home. Rico can train them as well as the horses we have. They'll take more time, of course. They have to be gentled with a slow, kind hand. You might even want to help." His eyes twinkled at her.

"A father-daughter project?"

"We haven't had one for a while. You need something to occupy your spare time. All you do is read those medical journals. You might as well be doing something worthwhile...until an adoption comes through."

Her father had always known how much the child she'd lost had meant to her, and she'd told him when she'd gone through the process of filling out papers and being approved as an adoptive parent.

He added, "When it happens, why don't you consider moving back in here with me. I've got this huge house to roam around in, and a kid should be around horses."

"Oh, Dad, thanks for offering, but I don't even know if an adoption's going to come through. It might not be for another year or more. Besides, would you really want a child getting into your prized possessions, making noise, being up all hours of the night?"

After a long hesitation, he admitted, "I'd like this house filled with laughter again."

She stood and looked into her father's eyes that were as blue as hers. His face was weathered from years of riding horses in the sun. At almost six feet tall, and even with his thinning hair and lined visage, he could be imposing if he wanted to be.

"If I do adopt, if I'm blessed with a child, I promise we'll be here every weekend, and you'll hear laughter in the house again."

She could have sworn his eyes grew a little misty, but he harrumphed, turned away from her and crossed to his desk. "Should I pencil you in on my calendar for the day of the auction?"

"You can pencil me in. If no emergencies crop up, I'll be glad to go with you."

"You sure you won't be too busy helping out Vince Rossi?" he asked slyly.

"I'm sure."

He pulled out his high-backed desk chair and sat in it, scribbling on the calendar on his desk. When he was done, he wheeled to face her. "Don't set your heart down in front of his boots. Don't let him trample it again."

"I'll be careful," she promised. "I'm not a teenager anymore."

"No, you're not. But where he's concerned, I'm not sure you have any common sense."

"You don't know the man Vince has become. Don't make judgments."

"And you're saying you *do* know him?"

"I know what I've seen, Dad. Actions always speak louder than words. He gave up his life—a life I think he liked—to take in this little boy. He's changing it all around for him and he's doing a good job. Nothing and no one is more important to him than Sean. He's doing what every good parent should, putting his child first."

"That's right. A good parent does put his child first, whether the child likes it or not."

Tessa shook her head. There were many things she and her dad would never agree on, but there were many things they did. She never doubted his love for her and she hoped he never doubted her love for him.

"So how about some gin rummy before I leave?" she offered.

"Are you still trying to win back the five hundred thousand toothpicks you owe me?"

"Better take a look at your records. I think I only owe you four hundred and twenty-five thousand now."

Her dad laughed and pulled open his desk drawer to find a deck of cards. Tessa knew she was using a card game with her dad as a distraction. If she went home, she'd think about Vince. She'd relive his lips on hers as well as his hands on her skin. She wondered how Sean was today. She wanted to call, but she wouldn't. *Don't set your heart down in front of his boots,* her father had warned her.

That was advice she was going to try to take.

* * *

Vince was concentrating on the duty roster Monday afternoon when Ginny buzzed him. "There's a Janet Fulton on the line. She says she's Sean's great-aunt."

Vince had e-mailed Janet over the weekend telling her Sean's surgery had gone well. He'd included a couple of photos from before surgery. She'd replied that she'd received the pictures and she'd call in a few days to inquire about her great-nephew.

That's all it was, Vince told himself. She just wanted to make sure Sean hadn't suffered ill effects from the surgery.

"Hello, Janet."

"Vince. I'm sorry to bother you at work, but I want to make a decision about something and needed to talk to you."

Vince kept a lid on musing about what that decision could be. "It's okay, Janet. I have a few minutes."

"First of all, how's Sean?"

"He's well. As I mentioned, he has to wear the sling for three weeks and we won't be able to start real physical therapy until then. He's energetic and alert and tries to crawl with one arm."

"Soon he'll be walking simply because it's easier."

"Could be."

After a pause, Janet said, "The reason I'm calling is that my vacation is coming up—I have a month—and I thought this might be a good time to visit you and look in on Sean."

At sixty, Janet had worked at an art gallery in Santa Fe most of her adult life. She'd never been particularly close to Scott and Carol, but maybe she regretted that now. Vince knew he had to tread carefully. After all, Janet was his son's only living relative. "You're welcome to come, of course, but I don't know if I can show you around, with my position as chief of police being temporary and having already taken time off for Sean. And I'm working some overtime."

"I see. Well, instead of being a burden, I'm sure I can help."

"Help?"

"Yes. I can take some of the responsibility for Sean off your shoulders. You said you have a housekeeper-nanny, but if you're spending more time at work, I'm sure she'd prefer a break, too."

If he told Janet that Rhonda had slipped into the mode of grandmother for Sean, she might resent the fact. He didn't know Janet Fulton very well so he wasn't exactly sure how to handle her.

"When were you thinking about coming?"

"The week after next. I'm going to rent a car so you don't have to worry about picking me up at the airport. I want to be able to get around on my own. I made reservations at a delightful bed-and-breakfast that gave me a week-to-week rate—the Blue Bonnet Inn. I spoke with the innkeepers, a retired couple who seem very nice."

"I have a spare bedroom," he offered reluctantly.

"Oh no, I don't want to impose or disturb your routine. I plan to be a tourist while I'm there. I've never been to Texas. So I'll be in and out."

In and out. No, she wouldn't be disrupting his life at all. "If you change your mind and want me to meet your flight, just let me know."

"I'll e-mail you when I finalize everything. But I think I'd prefer to rent a car and be on my own."

After, "It was good talking to you," and a friendly goodbye, they hung up.

Vince felt as if a lead stone had settled in his gut. Was Janet really just coming for a visit? Or was she coming to inspect his life with Sean?

If so, would it pass inspection?

Tessa wasn't surprised to see Vince and Sean on her appointment list Tuesday morning after a follow-up with Dr. Rafferty concerning the baby's surgery. It was always a good idea for the parent to touch base with the child's pediatrician. She was, however, surprised to see the worried look on Vince's face, the frown lines between his brows.

After Tessa examined Sean, she let him play with the plastic dinosaur Vince had brought along for him. It was meant to keep him occupied while she checked him over.

"He came through surgery with flying colors," she told Vince, hoping to allay any of his fears or worries.

"I can tell he can't wait to get that sling off. I can understand that." Vince paced back and forth in the small room.

"You're all set for physical therapy?" she asked.

"All set. We have an appointment July sixth." He continued to pace.

"Vince, what's wrong?"

He stopped and looked surprised that she'd noticed.

"You're as agitated as a horse cooped up in his stall for too long. Do you have concerns about Sean?"

"You don't have time for this," he said, going to his son and scooping him up into his arms.

She didn't know exactly what had gotten into her, especially after her conversation with her dad, but she crossed to only a step away from him. "I have time."

He blew out a breath and rocked Sean a bit to keep him happy. "His great-aunt is coming to visit next week. The only thing is, I don't think it's a visit. She's coming to keep tabs on me, what kind of father I am, how Sean is relating to me."

"She told you this?"

"She didn't have to. If I don't cover all the bases, she could try to take him away from me. I won't let that happen."

Tessa remembered finding out she was pregnant at seventeen, being thrust into parenthood feeling totally unprepared. Was that how Vince still felt? "What makes you think she'd have grounds?"

Frown lines etched Vince's brow. "Maybe I'm not with Sean as many hours as I should be. Maybe I rely on Rhonda too much. Maybe the condo isn't big enough, airy enough. Maybe I don't have enough diapers. How in the hell should *I* know?"

"She might just be coming for a visit," Tessa suggested calmly. Vince usually kept his emotions in check, maintained a calm exterior. He *must* be stressed.

"I have a gut feeling about this, and I can trust my gut."

Trying to be helpful, Tessa asked, "Do have the condo baby-proofed? The cabinets baby-locked or empty of anything he could hurt himself with?"

"Of course I do, and I've got enough food for the next year. Rhonda makes sure everything's clean. I don't think he needs more toys. I'm not worried about that. I'm worried about the things that matter. Am I doing those? How's a real father supposed to act? What would a real dad do with his son at this age?"

"Whoa!" Her gaze met his and didn't waver. "You *are* a real dad, Vince. You play with Sean, don't you? You do his exercises with him. You feed him when you're home. Those are all the things you should be doing."

"What else?"

She thought about it. "There is something that moms sometimes do to socialize their babies. Can you find an hour or two during the week to spend with Sean and with other children and their parents?"

"I'll find the hour or two. Where do I go and what do I do?"

Tessa almost smiled. Vince had always been a bottom-line, give-me-the-direct-route kind of person. "Let me make some inquiries. We have parent-and-child groups that meet here at Family Tree. I'll get a list for you, and you can see which one fits into your schedule the best."

"I know I've said this before, Tessa, but I am grateful for your help."

She really hadn't helped that much. She'd just shown him which way to turn. "If you just do what you've been doing, if you put Sean's concerns first, his great-aunt will have nothing to complain about."

Vince tenderly ruffled his baby's hair, then hiked him to his shoulder. "I hope that's true. My life is very different now than it used to be. I love Sean and I'm going to fight for him."

The intensity and passion she'd always loved in Vince was flaring high right now. She could understand his wanting to fight for Sean, for a different life and a home for the two of them. But she had to wonder. Why hadn't he fought for their marriage? Why hadn't he fought for their future? Had he not loved her enough? Had he loved her at all? Or had he simply felt it was his duty to marry her and to take over the responsibility of a child? Had she been so mistaken about the life they could have had?

There was no point wondering about it now. There was no point trying to relive what couldn't be rewritten.

Now it was Vince's turn to ask, "What's wrong?"

There was no way she was going to tell him what she'd been thinking. She glanced at her watch. "I don't want to be late for my next patient."

Vince's jaw set and he patted Sean's back. "I won't hold you up. I didn't mean to take up so much of your time."

She was quick to assure him, "Vince, it's all right. I told you, I'll help you any way I can."

They were walking a tightrope between the past and the future, between being friends and being more, between not being involved and falling over the cliff into something that had hurt them before.

Yet she couldn't let Vince leave with him thinking she didn't care, with him thinking that Sean was just another patient. "When Sean's great-aunt arrives, if there's anything I can do, don't hesitate to call me. I mean it, Vince."

After a long look, he gave a nod, said, "I'll keep that in mind," and left the office.

Tessa doubted that he'd call her again. He'd always had plenty of pride and that pride was one of the reasons their marriage had broken up.

With a sad feeling wrapping around her heart, Tessa picked up Sean's chart and carried it out to the receptionist.

At twelve forty-five on Friday, Tessa walked down the hall of the Family Tree Health Center to one of the community rooms. When she peeked in the door, she saw everyone gathered in a large circle. It didn't surprise her that Vince was there *and* he was the only man. The group had been in session since noon and if he'd been uncomfortable at the start, he didn't look uncomfortable now!

Tessa had suspected this might be the group Vince attended since the session fell over the lunch hour. With one foot in the door, she was ready to wave to the social worker in charge when she saw the woman beside Vince lean toward him. She whispered something in his ear, and he laughed. Sean was sitting on the floor in front of him. Her little red-haired girl crawled on the floor in front of her. The woman, who had beautiful red hair as well, was petite with a cute-as-a-button face. Tessa estimated her age to be about twenty-five.

With a smile still on his face, Vince didn't even hesitate to talk to her, to pass a fist-size ball to her little girl who looked to be about one. The toddler offered the ball to Sean and Sean tried to take it with his good hand.

"Tessa, come on in," Sophie Hodgekins invited her from the center of the circle. Sophie turned to everyone there. "Tessa's our resident pediatrician. She comes to the group now and then to help out."

Tessa shook her head so Sophie would realize she didn't have time for that today.

"You have five minutes to come in and say hi," Sophie persuaded. "You wouldn't have come up here otherwise."

She shouldn't have come at all. She should have just stayed away.

Reluctantly entering the room, she smiled at everyone including Vince. He gave her a nod and she crossed to him. "I came to see if you made it to a group," she said honestly.

"As you can see, we did."

The woman next to him extended her hand to Tessa. "I'm Lucy Atkins. Vince was telling me he's chief of police and I just couldn't believe that he'd take time off to bring his son in here. Isn't that wonderful?"

Vince's face had become stoically removed. Tessa knew he didn't like to be the center of attention, or the butt of praise. He never showed embarrassment, though, just became very stonelike. She could tell the woman liked Vince and was probably attracted to him. Tessa didn't see a wedding ring on her finger.

"Single dads can have a rough time of it. I thought the support group might help," Tessa said, filling in the silence.

"Support group?" Vince asked, frowning.

Tessa knew if she'd called it that before, he never would have come.

"Single moms have a hard time, too," Lucy interjected. "My divorce left me reeling. Then I turned up pregnant and my ex still didn't care. I told Vince we should make a playdate for our kids."

If Tessa could put into words what she felt at that moment, she'd have to admit she was three shades of jealous. She just couldn't help it. She hated the idea of Vince being with another woman. How stupid was that?

"Playdates are great for everyone getting to know each other," she suggested lamely, trying to keep up her end of the conversation while just wanting to run to the exit.

"I don't see this as a support group," Vince said, returning to the earlier subject. "It's just a place where parents can learn what kind of play is best for their kids, and how we can educate them as well as have fun. Right, Lucy?"

"Oh, absolutely. And while the kids play, we can exchange recipes." She threw Vince a coy look. "But in your case, I can just make you something and bring it over."

Vince wasn't accepting her offer, but he wasn't backing away, either. Tessa didn't know what to think. Was he attracted to Lucy?

Lifting Sean from the floor and into his arms, Vince motioned to the table with zwieback cookies for the kids and coffee for the adults. "I'm going to grab a cookie for Sean."

He looked at his son. "Want a cookie to chew on? Maybe you can make more teeth happen."

Tessa knew Sean had three new teeth and always had his finger in his mouth, gnawing on it, hoping to produce more.

Purposely Tessa didn't follow Vince. Instead, she mumbled an excuse about having something to talk to Sophie about and headed for the social worker.

But as soon as she approached Sophie, the leader of the group grinned at her. "You must have suggested that Chief Rossi come to our group to create some interest. I bet we'll have twice as many moms here next time. To see the chief of police as a dad isn't an everyday occurrence."

"I thought this would help...Sean," Tessa offered.

"Oh, I'm sure it will. But it should also help Vince with any public relations problems. These women will go out and spread the word that he might be a law-and-order guy, but he's gentle and caring with his son. I think Lucy is already seeing dual strollers in her future."

The idea of Vince walking down the street, pushing a stroller with another woman, cut Tessa to the quick. She absolutely hated the thought. However, she shouldn't because *she* couldn't give him children. He was a wonderful dad and he deserved to have many more kids. Yet she wasn't the woman who could give them to him—not now, not ever.

"What's wrong, Tessa?" Sophie asked with concern. "You went pale."

"Oh, nothing's wrong. I didn't grab lunch yet. My sugar's probably a little low. I've got to get back."

"I'd love it if you'd give a fifteen-minute nutrition talk to this group soon."

With Vince in the group? Watching Lucy flirt with him? "I don't know, Sophie. I'll have to check my schedule. I'll give you a call when I can free up some time. Maybe one of the other physicians in my practice could help out."

Sophie gave her an odd look as if she was surprised by Tessa's reluctance. "Okay, just let me know," she said agreeably.

Tessa headed for the door, intending to make a quick getaway, but suddenly Vince was there, stopping her. "Thanks for suggesting this."

She tried to keep her voice light. She swiped a crumb from Sean's little face as he gnawed on the zwieback. "So *you're* going to have a cookie for lunch, too?"

He chuckled. "I'll find a drive-through on my way back to the station after I take Sean home. With all the stimulation here, he's probably going to take a long nap this afternoon."

"It looks like you got a lot of stimulation, too." Once the words were out, she couldn't believe she'd said them.

He nodded toward all of the women in the group. "They're a talkative bunch, ready to swap war stories and anything else." Then with a look over his shoulder, he added, "Especially Lucy. She's had it tough on her own."

"She told you all about it?"

"Pretty much. That's a real shame her husband walked out on her. I can't believe any man would do that with a woman pregnant."

With a woman pregnant.

Tessa found she simply couldn't speak. Ever since her hysterectomy, she'd come to accept the fact she wouldn't have kids. Although she wanted to adopt, she gave her time and attention to her career and her practice and her little patients. But now the full impact of not having children hit her and hit her hard.

"Tessa?" Vince asked when she didn't respond.

Again she concentrated on Sean, only Sean, and tried to

pull air into her lungs. He was such an adorable little boy and her heart hurt for the little boy she'd lost. At this moment, the grief was as fresh as it had been twenty years ago.

Laying her hand gently on Sean's head, dragging her thumb across his brow, looking into his sweet face, she felt a lump in her throat that wasn't going to go away easily.

Her pride helped her manufacture a smile, helped her raise her chin, helped her meet Vince's eyes. "I'm glad this worked out for you."

"Vince," Lucy called. "I found my calendar. We can set up a playdate."

Before Vince could head for Lucy and a relationship that could progress as fast as both of them might want it to, Tessa said, "I hope all goes well with Sean's great-aunt. I'll be thinking about you and wishing you luck."

Then she left the community room and practically ran down the hall, heading for the stairs instead of the elevator. She needed the physical activity. She needed to work off feelings she didn't want to carry around with her all day. But she knew she'd be thinking about Lucy and Vince together and the picture of a typical happy family they could make together.

That lump closed her throat again, but Tessa took a deep breath and ran up the stairs.

Chapter Eight

Vince hadn't called her.

She hadn't called him.

Tessa hated to admit it, but she felt as if something was missing from her life even though she'd last seen Vince less than two weeks ago.

I'm just concerned about Sean, she told herself.

But then she dialed his number.

Vince answered with more of a bark than a hello.

"Vince?" she asked, not sure it was him.

"Tessa, hold on a minute." There was a long pause and then he was back on the phone, but she could hear Sean crying. "I really can't talk."

"Is something wrong with Sean?"

"No, nothing a little attention wouldn't fix. But I thought I could do this myself. Janet's coming over for supper. I scorched the rice. The asparagus are waterlogged, and I'm not

sure the hamburger steaks are edible. This is *really* going to
impress her. You wouldn't have a box of instant rice on hand
you could send by carrier pigeon, would you?"

"Actually I do have some in my pantry. Do you want me
to drop it by?"

There was silence. "You don't have anything better to do?
I don't like the idea of you pulling me out of a jam again."

"By dropping off instant rice?"

He blew out a breath. "Look…here…here's your dinosaur."

Sean stopped crying.

"I'm the chief of police," Vince announced to her. "I'm not
supposed to get into jams."

She had to laugh out loud at that one. "This is the real
world, Vince."

"If this dinner weren't so damn important—"

"If you don't want me to drop by, you can heat up a can
of baked beans."

After a few moments of silence, he asked, "Do you really
want to get involved? Meet Janet? Stay for dinner?"

She *really* hadn't thought that far ahead. "Do you *want* me
to get that involved?"

"Honestly, I don't know. Why don't you bring over the rice
and we'll go from there."

Ten minutes later, Vince was letting Tessa into his condo.
He still wore his uniform—white oxford, bolo tie and navy
slacks. He was jiggling Sean in one arm, his hair was disheveled, his shirt was rumpled and he looked ready to fight a bear.

Tessa handed Vince the box of rice and held her hands out
to Sean. "Come here, big boy." Sean was wearing clothes that
had seen a good part of his supper.

"I wanted to feed him so he'd play while Janet and I were
eating, but I think I got more on him than inside of him.

Babies and hurry-up don't go well together." Vince gave her one of those crooked grins that always melted her toes. "I've got to change him before I do anything else."

"Do you want me to do that?" she asked helpfully, not knowing if Vince wanted her to do anything at all.

"You don't mind?"

"Of course not. It will give me some time with him." She looked up at Vince. "I've missed him."

I missed you, too was hanging in the air between them but she didn't vocalize that thought. Rather, she took Sean to his bedroom to change him.

When she returned to the kitchen, Vince had started a batch of rice in the microwave. "I hope you can't tell this from the real thing."

"That depends on what we can cover it with."

He turned the broiler off. "I thought hamburger steaks would be easy. I should have bought a grill. I think they're leather."

Tessa set Sean in his high chair and peeked into the oven. The hamburger steaks were done but not past saving. "I can make gravy. We can use that with the rice, too. It should save the steaks if she gets here within fifteen minutes. What did you do for dessert?"

"I was smart and bought an apple pie at the diner."

They both laughed, their gazes held and Tessa suddenly felt breathless.

Breaking eye contact, she lifted the lid on the asparagus and shook her head. "Do you happen to have any more of these?"

"Actually I do. They're fresh ones."

"Great. We can roast them in the oven to add pizzazz to the meal. Grab a flat pan. I just need some olive oil, salt and pepper and garlic powder, if you have it."

Tessa was whisking gravy into the right consistency when

she asked, "What made you ever decide to invite Janet here for dinner? Rhonda could have cooked."

"I guess it was stupid but I wanted to do it myself. Mothers do it all the time. I wanted her to see I could handle Sean and provide everything he needs."

"You're providing everything he needs by having Rhonda look after him and cook."

"That's not the same thing," Vince muttered.

With high personal standards, Vince was a perfectionist. But with a job and a child, he had to learn to delegate. She stopped stirring and clasped his forearm. Somehow she needed to make him understand. "You have to choose what you do best and get help with the rest. New moms who work run into these problems all the time. They bring their kids in to me and feel guilty because they're not at home when their child is sick. You and I both know we don't live in a perfect world. We do what we have to do to get by."

It suddenly dawned on her that that's what she'd been doing all these years—getting by. She hadn't let herself think of Vince. She hadn't gotten involved in relationships. She hadn't wanted to take any risks.

Vince's expression gentled and his eyes went smoky. "Having you here tonight means a lot to me, Tessa."

She heard the sincerity in his voice, and she knew that look in his eyes. If she took a step closer to him—

The doorbell rang, breaking the moment, reminding Tessa why she was there.

After a few heartbeats, Vince went to the door.

Tessa could hear the exchange.

"I'm glad you could come," Vince said.

"I hope you didn't go to any trouble."

The two of them came into the kitchen.

Tessa smiled at Sean's great-aunt, who looked elegant in pale yellow linen slacks and a cream silk shirt. She was a strawberry blonde, her eyes blue like Sean's. She seemed to be at a loss when she saw Tessa.

Vince made the introductions. "Janet, this is Tessa McGuire, a friend of mine. I hope you don't mind if she joins us."

Janet looked from Vince to Tessa. "No, of course not. Do you often dine with Vince?" she asked Tessa.

Tessa gave the gravy one last stir. "We're old friends. We knew each other back in high school."

Vince's eyebrows shot up at that.

Janet seemed to absorb what Tessa had said as she went to Sean's high chair and asked, "May I lift him out?"

"He's a pretty friendly guy," Vince told her. "I don't think he'll mind. He likes freedom instead of confinement."

Laughing, Janet removed the tray in front of the baby and lifted him from his chair, careful of his arm and shoulder. "Haven't you gotten to be a big boy! Your pictures don't do you justice." She set her attention on Vince again. "His shoulder's coming along all right?"

"We're going to physical therapy once a week, but I do exercises with him every day."

"Once a week is enough?" she asked as if it wasn't.

"His physical therapist thinks so. Tessa is his pediatrician. She might be able to give you more insight if you'd like to ask her any questions."

Sitting in one of the kitchen chairs, nestling Sean on her lap, Janet said approvingly to Tessa, "So you're a doctor?"

"I sure am."

Vince motioned Tessa to the table beside Janet. "I'll set out dinner. Janet, do you drink coffee or tea?"

"Tea, thank you." She seemed impressed that he'd offered.

In a matter of minutes, Vince had supper on the table. Everything had turned out surprisingly edible.

"This is good," Janet concluded, finishing off another bite of hamburger steak topped with gravy. "Did Tessa make it, or did you?" she asked Vince.

"Let's just say I don't have problems making hamburger steaks or microwaving rice. It's when I have to have it all done at the same time that it becomes a problem. Tessa helped with the timing and roasted the asparagus."

Again, Janet looked from one of them to the other, then at little Sean sitting in his high chair, stuffing bits of rice into his mouth, along with some of his favorite cereal.

"Am I going to meet your housekeeper while I'm here?" Janet asked.

"Rhonda is here every day with Sean while I'm at work. You're welcome to stop in."

"She won't mind if I barge in?" Janet inquired.

Before Vince could answer, the cell phone on his belt beeped. He checked the caller ID and then said, "Excuse me. I have to take this."

After a few curt sentences asking the caller when and where, he closed his phone and rubbed his forehead. "I'm going to have to leave. There was a fire in a restaurant in town and I need to be on the scene. I can call Rhonda—"

Tessa shook her head. "I can stay as long as you need me to. Go ahead, we'll be fine." Tessa reached over to Sean and wiped a kernel of rice from his mouth.

"Yes, of course we'll be fine," Janet echoed. "I can play with Sean, and with his pediatrician here, I'll know exactly what to do and what not to do. Do you get called away like this often?"

"Whenever necessary," Vince stated matter-of-factly. Crouching down to Sean, he rubbed his son's hair and kissed him on the cheek. "I'll be back as soon as I can, buddy. Don't give Tessa or Aunt Janet any trouble, okay?"

Sean waved his hand at Vince and babbled in baby talk.

Vince said to Janet, "If I'm not back by the time you leave, I'll give you a call tomorrow."

Sean's great-aunt nodded, her gaze on Vince's back as he hurried out the door.

"He didn't even get to eat half his supper. How often does this happen?" she asked Tessa.

"I really can't say, Mrs. Fulton. I do know Rhonda is on call for whenever he has to leave."

"Does she center her life around Vince and Sean?"

"She's very fond of them both and considers them like family."

"But she isn't family, is she?"

"Family means different things to different people. She doesn't have blood ties, but she couldn't care more if Sean was her own grandchild."

Janet pushed around a spear of asparagus on her plate. "Vince established himself here particularly fast, don't you think?"

"Sagebrush was his hometown. He brought Sean back here because there's a specialist in Lubbock."

"Tell me something, Tessa. Exactly why did Vince have you here tonight? Moral support?"

"He ran out of rice."

Janet's eyes widened. "You aren't serious."

"I am. I called to see how Sean was doing. He explained you were coming for dinner and he'd burned the first batch of rice."

"The way you two look at each other, I thought maybe you were here every night."

How to answer *that* one. What would Vince want her to say? The truth was, if Janet Fulton dug deep enough or asked enough questions, she'd soon find out on her own. "Vince and I married as soon as we graduated from high school. But we lost a baby and it didn't work out."

Janet's surprise was obvious and made her pause. Finally, she asked, "You were in touch all of these years?"

"No, we weren't. It was a coincidence that Vince turned up at my practice with Sean…or fate. And now we're working at just trying to be friends."

Friends with benefits? a little voice in Tessa's head asked, remembering each vivid detail of every kiss.

"I…see," Janet murmured thoughtfully.

But Tessa knew Janet couldn't really see because she herself couldn't see clearly. She was more attracted to Vince than she'd ever been to any man but she didn't want just the proverbial roll in the hay. That's all that could happen between them, wasn't it? He didn't believe he knew how to be a husband. There was a world of hurt between them. She'd be staying and he'd be leaving.

No, she didn't see anything about Vince clearly.

Vince returned home around midnight. When Tessa saw him, she asked, "Are you okay?"

His white shirt was streaked with soot. There was a smudge below his eye and soot on his forearms.

He took off his Stetson, dusted it against his leg, and then hung it on the hook behind the door. "The wind was blowing my way."

"Was it bad?"

"Bad enough. At first we were afraid the volunteer fire company couldn't put it out. I was ready to call Lubbock but then the wind died down and a few more men arrived. The restaurant's history now. It's a shame."

"What caused it?"

"The fire marshal from Lubbock is examining the scene. They're talking to the owners and the witnesses. It sounded as if it started in the storeroom. My guess is old electrical wiring sparked and caught."

"They were open for business?"

"No, thank goodness. They're closed for vacations. Did Sean go down okay?"

"He was a sweetie. Janet and I both sang him lullabies. She's really good with him."

"I don't think I want to hear this," Vince grumbled as he unbuttoned his shirt and shrugged out of it.

Tessa swallowed hard. All that tanned skin, black chest hair, well-developed muscles.

"I need to get a quick shower," he said. "I suppose you have to go. Do you have rounds in the morning?"

"Yes, I do, so I should be on my way. But, Vince, I think you need to know something first."

He tossed his shirt to the counter and came closer to look at her more carefully. "What do I need to know? Did Janet say something about the way I'm raising Sean?"

"No, nothing like that. In fact, I really do think she was impressed, at least she seemed to be. She also seemed sincere and that's why…"

"Why what?"

"She asked me a few questions. My being here aroused her curiosity and then of course I mentioned we knew each other in high school. So she wanted to know if we were dating or anything like that."

Vince's brow furrowed. "And?" he prompted.

"I told her we married after we graduated from high school."

His astonishment drew lines around his mouth. "Why would you tell her *that?*"

"Because it's not a deep, dark secret. If she digs around at all, she'd find out. Do you want her to think we're keeping it from her?"

Tessa knew that look in Vince's eyes. He wanted to blow up or rant and rave, but he wouldn't. Calm control took over.

"Don't shut down like that," Tessa protested.

"I'm not shutting down. I'm trying to hold on to my temper. She doesn't need to know every detail of my life!"

"Vince, I'm sorry. I thought being up front about us was best."

He raked his hand through his hair. "I get that. It's just— I know now how you felt about my leaving for the Air Force. I don't want her to think we didn't try."

"We *didn't* try, did we?"

"We *tried,* Tessa. We tried before you lost the baby. We never should have gotten married and you know it. I don't want Janet thinking that because our marriage didn't work out, I'd leave Sean for some reason. Our situation was complicated but my taking on the responsibility of Sean isn't. He needs me and I'll never forsake the responsibility that Scott and Carol bestowed on me."

Their situation had been complicated. But why hadn't he been this committed to her? Because he knew her father would support her and be glad Vince was gone from her life? "Maybe you should be telling *her* that," Tessa replied, holding in past hurt to deal with the present situation.

"Maybe I will. I'm sure I'll be seeing more of her."

Tessa fought to stay in the present. "I think she'd really like to babysit for Sean while she's here—all alone without someone looking over her shoulder."

"If I let her do that, she could become really attached to him. You know what I'm afraid of, Tessa? I don't want her thinking she can take him back with her."

"She knows you're his legal guardian."

"And she's his great-aunt."

"Just think about it," Tessa prompted.

"I will."

There were only mere inches between them, and they gazed at each other, neither looking away. "If I kiss you again," he asked, "will you run?"

"If you kiss me again," she said truthfully, "I might not make it in time to the hospital tomorrow morning to make rounds and I have a full day of appointments."

"So what would happen if I asked you to stay when you didn't have a full day of appointments?"

What was she saying and doing? Something had happened tonight and she wasn't sure what—some subtle shift in her relationship with Vince. A shift that scared her.

"We both have an early day tomorrow," she murmured. "Maybe we should just leave it at that."

Vince took a step back. "Whatever the lady wants. Thanks for the help with the gravy and asparagus."

"Maybe sometime I'll make you one of my home-cooked dinners," she teased.

"I'd like that."

Before the aforementioned kiss could become a reality, she picked up her purse and headed for the door. "Have a good weekend, Chief."

"You, too, Dr. McGuire. I'll be in touch."

When she left Vince's home, she couldn't help but wonder when and where he'd be in touch. She couldn't help being excited about the thought of seeing him again.

* * *

"What do you think?" Tessa asked Vince Saturday afternoon, holding up jeans and a red knit shirt with a football embroidered in the center. She'd been inordinately pleased when Vince had called her earlier in the afternoon and asked her if she wanted to go shopping with him for some new clothes for Sean. He was letting Janet spend some alone time with her nephew.

"I think you already have more outfits in your arm than he can wear in a year."

Tessa looked down at everything she'd picked up. The children's store was like one great big candy shop and she was having the time of her life. "Are you telling me he doesn't need a new outfit for every day of the week?" she teased with a grin.

"He needs a couple of pairs of shorts and a few shirts."

She shook her head. "Men! No sense of style." She pointed to the baby shoes lined up on a shelf. "What about a pair of sneakers?"

"Sneakers are good," Vince agreed, coming up beside her and dropping his arm around her shoulders.

In that moment, she wasn't only attracted to his scent and his strength and his sense of responsibility where Sean was concerned. She was also attracted to his sense of humor, his ability to see past the obvious, his stubbornness and his gentleness. With his arm around her while they were buying clothes for Sean, she felt almost giddy and knew that was dangerous. If she started dreaming of a life with Vince again, would her effort bring her joy or more pain?

He found a pair of sneakers in Sean's size and added them to her pile. Under the brim of his Stetson, his eyes darkened and he looked as if he wanted to kiss her, right there in the baby store.

A chiming sound suddenly came from Tessa's purse.

"Are you on call?" Vince asked.

"No, but one of the docs could need something." She handed her pile of clothes to Vince, fished out the phone and opened it. She hesitated only a moment and then put it to her ear. "Dad?"

She saw the tightening of Vince's jaw, the lines cutting deep around his eyes.

"Tessa," she heard her father rasp. "I fell—"

"I can hardly hear you. Did you say you fell? Where?"

"Rico is off today. I saddled up Aztec and rode him down to the creek. We were doing fine until a jackrabbit poked out of a dagblasted hole."

"Where at the creek?"

"Near the three cottonwoods."

"Should I call an ambulance?"

Vince stepped closer to her.

"No! No ambulance. I don't think I broke anything. I just can't put weight on my knee."

"Isn't anyone around the ranch so I can give them a heads-up?"

"No one's around right now."

"Where's Aztec?"

"He's right here, looking guilty like he did something wrong. But he didn't. He's not going anywhere. He's a loyal one."

"Keep your phone in your hand and stay connected to me. You aren't in the sun, are you?"

"No, ma'am. I dragged myself into the shade. I do have *some* common sense."

"I'll be there as soon as I can, Dad. Hold on a minute, okay?" She looked up at Vince. "My dad took a tumble off

Aztec down by the creek. I have to go get him. I don't know if I'll be able to get him into the car by myself."

"You want me to come along?" He looked stunned.

"If you don't want to, I'll call one of the docs I know."

She could see Vince was imagining seeing Walter McGuire again. The idea obviously didn't sit well with him.

"I'll go with you," he decided curtly.

"Dad, I'm bringing help," she said over the phone.

"Who?" her father asked suspiciously.

"I'm with Vince. We'll be there as soon as we can."

"Damn it all, Tessa. He's the last person I want help from."

"Yeah, well, I'm not sure he's all that thrilled about it, either, but I don't see that you have a choice, do you?"

"Is this payback?" he growled.

"No, it's just us getting you out of a jam. Hold on to your phone."

Her father swore again, a little more vigorously this time.

"Do you think it's serious?" Vince asked, his eyes steely-gray.

"No way to know until I see him. As I said, if you don't want to go—"

"If I don't go with you, I'm obviously ducking karma. But if I do go with you, Tessa, there's no telling what will happen. I won't start anything, but you know your dad."

Yes, she did. She had no way to predict how he'd react to seeing Vince face-to-face again. No way at all.

Chapter Nine

"Dad's over there!"

Tessa motioned to the cluster of three cottonwoods as the pickup truck Vince drove rumbled over ruts and brush. They'd traded his SUV for her dad's vehicle at the barn because she knew it could handle the rough terrain.

When she stole a glance at Vince, she noted the hard set of his jaw. This encounter with her father wasn't going to be an easy meeting and they both knew it.

Handling the pickup expertly, Vince edged it as close as he could to the cottonwoods and to Walter McGuire. Aztec, a seventeen-hand bay gelding, wasn't far away. He was eyeing the pickup as if he recognized it.

"How do you want to play this?" Vince asked Tessa. "You're not going to get him to the pickup on your own steam."

"We can both help him, then you can drive Dad back to the house and I'll ride Aztec."

"*You'll* ride Aztec?"

"He spooks sometimes, but he'll be calm because he knows me. Besides, how long has it been since you rode a horse?"

"Not so long as you might think. I went riding in Albuquerque." He peered toward the trees. "We'll see what your dad has to say about the whole transportation scenario. He might not want me even driving his truck."

They exited the pickup and approached Walter McGuire. When they'd driven up, he'd been lying flat. Now he sat up and adjusted his Stetson on his head.

"Rossi," her father acknowledged tersely.

"Mr. McGuire," Vince returned, giving a bit of deference yet using the same curt tone.

Vince hunkered down next to Tessa's father. "There's more than one way to do this. Tessa could try to help you to your truck, but you could fall and damage your knee further. I'm sure I could get you there on my own, but if you're concerned I have something else besides your welfare on my mind, Tessa can help you on your good side and I'll help you on your bad one."

"You think you have this all figured out, don't you?" her father muttered.

"I don't have anything figured out, sir. We just got the call you needed help and here we are."

Her father gave Vince a sharp look, and she knew both men were wondering what the other was thinking.

"Let's get you out of the heat, Dad. If you and Vince want to have a conversation, you can do it back at the house." She lifted her father's wrist and took his pulse. Next, she put a stethoscope to her ears and listened to his heart.

"It's my knee, daughter."

She gently felt around the knee and when he jerked away,

she shook her head. "I think you did it this time. Arthroscopic surgery for sure."

"I think all doctors are sadists. They can't wait to make that incision and get inside."

"Only to fix something, Pop. I don't want you putting any weight on that leg."

Before Tessa envisioned what Vince was going to do, he counted, "One, two, three," and hiked her dad up to a standing position.

She quickly filled in on his other side.

"I need to take you to the E.R., Dad, and get an MRI."

"This isn't a good day," he grumbled.

"No day's a good day. We can ice your knee, but my guess is that it's going to swell and hurt like blazes."

"You have a crystal ball?" her dad asked acerbically.

"I have a lot of experience. I don't need a crystal ball," she shot back.

Realizing he might have hurt her professional pride, his tone gentled. "I have a pair of crutches from that fall I took a couple of years ago. I don't want to get into that whole rigmarole at the E.R. Let's just see what happens."

Tessa sighed. Once her father made up his mind, there was no changing it. "If the knee swells, I'll take you to the E.R. in the morning. In the meantime, Vince will drive you back. I'll ride Aztec in."

Her father looked as if he was going to protest and then he realized why she'd suggested it. "Yeah, Aztec knows you. I guess that's best."

"I'm sure I can handle him, Mr. McGuire, if you'll feel more comfortable with Tessa driving you."

"Since you *are* chief of police, I trust you handling my truck, rather than one of my prized horses."

When Tessa saw the scowl on Vince's face, she knew he and her dad were off to a bumpy start.

Fifteen minutes later, she and Vince had helped her dad to his favorite recliner in his den. "Why don't you go get us something to drink," her dad asked. "Me a shot of bourbon, Rossi here a beer or something if he wants it."

"No thanks, sir, I'm fine."

"You know where my good bourbon is in my office," he said to Tessa.

She took that as a cue to leave. The showdown had to take place without her, she supposed, though she'd give a month's salary to find out what the two of them had to say.

The silence in the room was as thick as the Persian carpet on the floor, Vince thought, as he considered how he was going to handle any conversation with this man.

"Ice on that knee might help," he suggested.

"You telling me what's good for *me?*" McGuire asked, going on the offensive.

"I was just making a suggestion," Vince countered calmly.

"You always did know how to be diplomatic…except with Tessa."

Vince could leap into this conversation or drag his feet. One way or the other he was sure it was going to go downhill. He leapt anyway. "I always tried to be honest with Tessa."

"Sometimes honesty is just an excuse to do what you want to do."

Vince knew exactly what McGuire meant. "At the hospital, you told me Tessa blamed me for everything that happened and you were right. She deserved a better life than I could give her. She made the choice to come home with you because she did blame me and she had everything she needed here."

McGuire frowned at that as if it wasn't quite the answer he'd expected. "That's what *I* thought. But she was miserable after you left and damn near fell apart. *You* on the other hand, as we heard, went skipping right along, got real chummy with someone on the base, discovered a career in a place you wanted to stay. I suppose you thought it was best for Tessa not to contact her, too?"

"If I had written her a letter, would you have given it to her?"

McGuire mulled that over. "I don't rightly know. What I do know is that no matter what she says, she's never gotten over what happened."

"You mean losing the baby and the hysterectomy?"

"I mean all of it. She was a strong girl and she's turned into a strong woman. She's a survivor. But I believe deep down, she's never forgiven *me* for interfering or *you* for breaking her heart."

There it was, the reason he and Walter McGuire would always be at odds. "I probably could never have understood what you felt before I had Sean. He's almost nine months old now. Has Tessa told you about him?"

"She told me a little."

"One day I was a bachelor, the next day I was a father. My best friend was gone and I had responsibility for his child. And it's more than a responsibility. That little guy owns my heart and if *anybody, anybody* at all ever tried to hurt him, I'd want to make sure they didn't. So maybe now I can understand how you feel about me and everything that happened."

McGuire looked away for a few moments as if to consider or absorb what Vince had said. When his gaze swung back to Vince's, it was piercing but not condemning. "So how does it feel to be chief of police in Sagebrush when your dad once inhabited its jail?"

Vince could have taken the comment as a slur, but he didn't. It was a fact. His dad had slept off more than one bender in the Sagebrush jail. "I could say one has nothing to do with the other, but that wouldn't be the truth. I went into law enforcement because my mother was murdered. I had the misguided idea I could right some kind of wrong."

McGuire arched a brow. "You can't?"

"I can try but the wrongs mount up awfully fast, and righting them seems to get harder and harder. In Sagebrush, it's easier than it was in Albuquerque, no doubt about that."

"You want easier?"

"No, sir, I don't. That's why this job is just temporary."

McGuire mulled that over, too, then rubbed his chin. "You want to go back to being a homicide detective?"

"I can't. Not now. Maybe when Sean's older. But I do want to work at a job that makes a difference."

"You can make a difference as chief of police."

"Farmer is coming back. This isn't my job to keep, even if I did want it."

"You're almost out," Tessa interrupted them cheerily from the doorway, holding up the bottle of bourbon. She clutched an ice pack in her other hand.

"You think I don't have a spare tucked away?" her father asked her with a twinkle in his eye that was obviously only for his daughter.

"I should have known. So what did I miss?" She brought over the bottle of bourbon with an old-fashioned glass turned upside down on top and set it on the table next to him, then she applied the ice pack to his knee.

"We were just catching up," McGuire explained with a glance at Vince. "Just catching up."

Vince wasn't sure if they'd accomplished anything in their

conversation or not, but at least they hadn't gone at each other like two gunfighters at noon. That didn't mean they wouldn't in the future. He and Walter McGuire had a history, and that history wouldn't be forgotten anytime soon.

Tessa poured two fingers of bourbon into the glass and handed it to her dad. "I think I should stay here tonight. If the knee's not better in the morning, I'll take you to the emergency room."

"I don't need anyone here," McGuire grumbled, casting a sideways glance at Vince.

Now Vince realized he had been hoping for an afternoon with Tessa, maybe even more than that. Yet today, instead of seeing a controlling father and a submissive daughter, he was seeing a relationship that was give and take. It had ups and downs. But most of all, he'd witnessed affection and caring.

Had the years made so much difference? Had Walter McGuire mellowed? Or had Vince seen what he'd wanted to see twenty years ago? Had he wanted his freedom and blamed Tessa for knowing that he did? Had he mistakenly believed that Tessa's choice to go home with her father hadn't been a real choice at all? Had she gone home with Walter McGuire to relieve Vince of duty and responsibility?

There were so many questions, questions with answers that could only cause them more pain.

Seeing this situation clearly for what it was, Vince put in his two cents. He said to McGuire, "You might not think you need anyone now, but if that knee swells up and you can't walk tonight, you could have a problem just getting to the bathroom."

"Great," McGuire grunted. "Two against one." But there wasn't a whole lot of protest behind it.

"Are there any chores you need to have done that are going to be a problem with that knee?" Vince asked.

"You have an hourly fee?" McGuire joked.

"No, sir. But if Tessa's watching over you, she really can't take care of the animals, too."

"Are you trying to start an argument?" Tessa's dad grumbled.

"I'm trying to help out. If you don't want the help, I'll leave."

McGuire swished his bourbon around in his glass, glanced at Tessa, Vince, then back at the bourbon.

He addressed Vince. "Do you still know your way around a horse?"

"I've handled animals over the years."

"Saddle-Up needs salve on his right eye. Daisy Mae will be foaling in about a week. Just make sure all's well with her and bring in the others. The weatherman's calling for storms tonight and I don't want them spooked. Tessa can show you where the feed is. In the morning, we'll feed them and let them out. Tim's boy is coming over after church and can do whatever else needs to be done."

"I'll go down to the barn with you and show you where everything is," Tessa offered. "Do you need anything else, Dad?"

Her father hiked himself up out of his chair, held on to the arm and hopped over to the sofa. "Just give me the remote control and I'll be fine."

Tessa did that and by the time she met Vince at the door, her dad was engrossed in the History Channel.

"Are you sure you have time for all of this?" she asked Vince as they left the house and started for the barn.

"I have time. I'll check in with Janet before I start with the horses, but I have a feeling she'd rather I come home later than sooner."

"She *is* good with Sean."

"Almost as good as you are."

When Tessa went silent, he knew she had to have mixed feelings about getting close to Sean, about a child she wished had been theirs. Whenever she was with Sean, he sensed she kept part of herself removed…just as she did from him.

Once inside the barn, Vince was surprised that good memories came rushing back. He'd met Tessa at the barn several nights after her dad had turned in. Those clandestine visits had been filled with excitement, longing and the ful-fillment they found in each other's arms.

Not only that, but he liked barns. He'd always relished being around horses, taking care of them, riding them. There was freedom in riding a horse that he hadn't found anywhere else. The scents of hay, sun-ripened wood and a musty damp-ness belonging to all barns filled him with the desire to purchase horses of his own someday. Wouldn't Sean love that? And he could so easily envision Tessa by his side…

Tessa showed Vince to the tack room. There were white metal cabinets located beside the desk. She opened one of the doors and took out a tube of medication, handing it to him. "For Saddle-Up's eye."

He slipped the tiny tube into his shirt pocket then moved closer to her. "This afternoon turned out differently than I'd planned."

"What had you planned?" she asked softly.

"A shopping trip. Maybe some necking in my SUV. Dinner, then maybe more necking, possibly at your house."

"Necking," she repeated and turned her eyes up to his. "We might have gone beyond that."

He slipped his hand under her hair. "We might have."

"Maybe it's a good thing my dad called."

He studied her for a long moment. "Why won't you just let yourself feel and enjoy?"

"Because feeling and enjoying are fine, but what comes after…"

The truth was, he didn't care about what came after. All he cared about was the need and hunger in Tessa's eyes that matched his. All he cared about was getting closer to her again. All he cared about was stepping away from the past and seeing what the present brought.

He bent to her and kissed her. Nothing could have stopped the surge of need that rushed through him.

Tessa didn't hesitate to reciprocate. Her tongue stroked his. As she pressed into him, her soft moan of pleasure told him she wanted more. But then she braced her hands on his chest and leaned away. When she looked up at him, her eyes were wide and vulnerable.

After taking a few moments to catch her breath, she said, "I have to know where we go from here. Are we just going to kiss and neck like teenagers, and at the end of August when your stint as chief is up, we'll go back to our lives the way they were before you came?"

Her question frustrated him. "Why can't you just accept *now?*"

"Because we had *now* once before and look what happened."

He raked his hand through his hair because he knew she was right. How could he make plans when Sean and his condition were his main concern, when finding a job wasn't as easy as choosing a career, when Sagebrush could be the last place on earth he wanted to stay?

"You won't move from Sagebrush, will you?" he demanded, remembering how the security her father had offered had torn them apart before.

"Not now. I can't. Dad could need me and I won't turn my back on him."

Those words meant something different to Vince today than they might have meant yesterday. Yesterday, he would have gotten angry, fallen back on the idea that Walter McGuire had always controlled Tessa and she would do what he said. But today, he knew there was real affection between the two of them as there should be between parent and child. He'd never known that kind of affection. Yet he felt it now for Sean and he understood how Tessa could feel it for her father.

How could Vince promise her more than "now"? How could he consider being the husband she needed when he'd failed at it once before? When he'd never had a role model to see how it should be done? Maybe that's what had kept him from staying twenty years ago. Maybe that's what kept him from moving them forward now. Tessa deserved someone who would put her first, romance her, court her, be steadfast and committed for the next fifty years. He didn't know if he was capable of that. For now he was committed to Sean and that's all he knew.

Tessa moved her hands from his chest and turned to the cabinet and closed it. Her hair slid along her face and covered her expression. "The feed bins are still around the corner and the horses' stalls have nameplates. Saddle-Up is third from the end."

As she headed for the tack room door, Vince wanted to catch her hand. But he didn't. Maybe it was best he let her go.

"If I'm not in the living room with Dad, I'll be in the pantry seeing what I can make for dinner. You're welcome to stay."

"I'll see how late it gets. I don't want Janet to become too at home with Sean."

Tessa nodded her understanding and left the barn.

Unbidden thoughts turned back twenty years. He remembered when Tessa had been six months pregnant, lugging groceries up the steps to their apartment. For a change he'd gotten home at a decent time and he'd run halfway down to help her. He'd taken the grocery sacks from her arms, directed her to stay right there and run them up to their dingy apartment. Then he'd hurried back down and swung her up into his arms.

"What are you doing?" she'd gasped.

They hadn't made love for a week. With his two jobs, he'd hardly seen her. "I'm saving you a few steps and welcoming you home. Tonight I'm going to make dinner."

She laughed. "What are you going to make?"

"I don't know, but whatever it is, it will be delicious, just like our lovemaking."

She'd smiled shyly. "I know I've fallen asleep the last couple of nights before you got home, but I didn't mean to. I want to make love with you, Vince. I want that more than anything."

One of the horses neighed and snapped Vince back to the present. They'd been kids, with roaring hormones and too much naiveté. Now they were realistic adults, and that's why Tessa had left the barn with only a taste of what their passion could deliver.

He had to make some decisions before he could move forward with her. He'd have to make sure the decisions were the right ones for both of them.

Late Sunday morning, Tessa registered her father and got him settled in the E.R. An MRI was being taken. Instead of just sitting in the waiting room, she decided to see how Amy

Garwin was before returning to wait for her father. The teenager had been on her mind more than she wanted to admit for many, many reasons. Tessa had stopped in her room a few times when she made rounds, but nothing had changed. Her family was hoping for a miracle and Tessa was, too.

Tessa tried not to think about Vince as she bought flowers at the gift shop then rode up the elevator. Last night she'd just wanted to cry. She'd walked out when she could have had paradise. But paradise for a night wasn't the paradise she envisioned. And even in paradise, she and Vince would have to come to terms with losing a baby Sean couldn't replace.

As she stepped off the elevator, she was surprised to see Vince at the end of the hall, speaking with two policemen. Without hesitating, she went toward him. The two patrolmen finished their conversation with him and passed her as they headed for the elevator.

"Trouble?" she asked, wondering why he was here.

"We had a DUI. He zigzagged from Sagebrush into Lubbock, hit two parked cars, so both jurisdictions were affected. The patient's blood alcohol was off the chart. Someone has to explain to him that if he's going to drink like this, he could end up dead or in prison. He was lucky he didn't injure anyone but himself."

"You're taking on the responsibility of confronting him?"

"He's forty-two, apparently with no family who cares. As soon as he's clearheaded enough to talk to me, I'm going to take a stab at it. In the meantime, I thought I'd visit Amy." He glanced at the bouquet of flowers in Tessa's hand. "I guess that's where you're going, too?"

"Yeah, I thought I'd give her family moral support if nothing else."

"Maybe we can both do that."

Maybe they could…together. Surprising them both, she linked her arm through Vince's. He looked down at her questioningly.

"Shouldn't I?" she asked. "Is it bad for your image?"

"The hell with my image. I just want to know what it means."

"It means I like you and we're friends and we're going to do this together."

He studied her carefully. "Are you nervous about visiting Amy?"

Vince could always read her too well. "A little. In the past, I've felt…extraneous. I want to make a difference, but I don't know if I can. Her family trusts me and I haven't been able to deliver, not any more than anybody else has."

Vince covered her hand with his. "All we can do is try."

When Tessa walked into Amy's room, she actually felt the love that surrounded the teenager. The room itself spoke of everything Amy cherished most. Pictures of her and her friends hung on the walls. There were photographs from a Halloween party, homecoming, a Christmas concert. Her favorite songs were playing on the CD player. Tessa knew her mom read her articles from the newspaper and her sister chattered about gossip from school. Her father, with several books on the cart beside the bed, had often read to Amy, trying to find that perfect something that would get through to his daughter.

After greeting the family, Tessa and Vince stood by Amy's bed, not sure what to say or do.

After a moment, Vince cupped Amy's shoulder. "Amy, you probably don't know my voice. I'm Vince Rossi, chief of police. You're mom's probably told you this, but your school-mates really miss you. Everybody misses you."

Only silence and stillness permeated the room. But Vince

went on anyway. "I remember what it was like to be seventeen and have the whole world ahead of me. You still have the whole world ahead of you, Amy. Can you give us some sign that you know we're here? We want you back with us."

Tessa could have sworn Amy's eyelids fluttered. She could have sworn that the teenager's little finger moved. Those could have been reflexive reactions, but were they?

Now Tessa stepped up to the bed on the other side of the teenager and took her hand. She spoke softly to her for a while as Vince had, mentioning the Great Chili Cook-off coming up on Saturday, recounting a story about one of her favorite horses at her dad's ranch.

Amy's mother's eyes were filled with understanding as Tessa ran out of things to say.

After a few more minutes of conversing with Amy's family, Tessa and Vince left.

Out in the hall, Tessa admitted to Vince, "I don't know how her mother stays with her, talks with her, eats with her, reads to her every single day without any response. That's got to be killing her."

"What else is she supposed to do, Tessa? Just let her daughter lie there and fade away?"

"No, but…" Tessa rubbed her temples, then looked up at Vince. "Could you do it?"

"Without a doubt. Even if it made no difference, I would try. Having a child is about doing everything and hoping something works."

They were at the stairwell now and Vince added, "It's sort of like being with you."

"Being with me?"

"I try a little bit of everything and hope something works."

After he studied her face a few moments, he asked, "How

about a real date? I'll pick you up after rounds tomorrow night. We can stop and see Amy together, then we can have dinner and just chill."

"Chill?"

"You *do* know what that means," Vince teased.

"I know it means to hang out with someone you're comfortable with."

"Exactly. We'll learn how to be so comfortable with each other that no situation will ever be awkward again."

She smiled, in spite of herself. "You almost have me believing it."

"Believe it. You can spend time with me, spend time with Sean, eat supper with us, just see what a night like that can be." His voice was calm and casual, suggesting something that almost seemed mundane.

But for Tessa there were pitfalls that could send her scurrying away. Wasn't it about time she grew up, accepted what was and saw what is? Vince was offering her the opportunity to be happy now, if not in the future. Life *was* short. Maybe she should just enjoy it. Maybe she should accept Vince just the way he was and go from there.

"All right," she suddenly agreed.

"All right?" he asked warily.

"You asked me out on a date, one where I'd feel comfortable. I'm accepting. Tomorrow night is good," she added softly.

She felt like a teenager again…feeling like that seventeen-year-old who'd believed in happily ever after.

Chapter Ten

Tessa returned home from the hospital to the sounds and smells of Emily and Francesca cooking in the kitchen. Tessa sniffed appreciatively, crossed to the stove and lifted the lid on the pot where stew was simmering.

"This looks wonderful. What's the occasion?" Tessa asked.

Francesca stood at the chopper and exchanged a look with Emily, who was slicing strawberries into a pie shell. "We needed something to do with our hands so we could keep our thoughts from scurrying into places we don't want them to go."

Tessa sighed. "I know what you mean."

"How's your dad?" Emily asked.

"As stubborn as ever. The doc says he needs arthroscopic surgery but Dad doesn't want to have it now. So he's going to take anti-inflammatory medication and see a physical therapist for a couple of sessions to learn exercises to strengthen the muscles."

"Will he be able to drive himself?" Francesca chopped tomatoes to add to the avocado.

"It's his left knee so he says he'll be able to. I talked to Rico and he says he'll be on standby in case Dad needs a driver. Is there anything you need me to do? I'd like to keep *my* hands busy, too."

"Salad," Emily suggested, giving Tessa a look. "Where are *your* thoughts going?"

"I ran into Vince at the hospital and we visited Amy. I just feel so bad for her and her family."

Crossing to the refrigerator, Tessa found the head of lettuce in the crisper drawer. She also grabbed carrots and a cucumber. Then she mentioned casually, "Vince and I are going on…a date tomorrow night."

Francesca stopped what she was doing.

"We're going to meet up after my rounds and I'll spend the evening with him and Sean."

"Cozy," Emily said. "I told Dr. Madison I'd stay late tomorrow night and help input patient records into the new system."

Tessa pulled a cutting board from a cabinet. "For professional reasons…or personal ones?"

Emily stiffened for a moment and then shrugged. "Both. When I'm around him, I can forget for a little while how Richard made me feel."

Emily rarely talked about her ex-husband or her marriage and her life before she came to Sagebrush, so Tessa paid attention. "I don't hear scuttlebutt around Family Tree about Dr. Madison. I've never heard anything about him dating. I think he concentrates on his twin daughters and his practice and that's about it."

"I know," Emily agreed. "And he's never made any indication that we have anything other than a professional relationship. He respects what I do. I respect what he does. But…"

"But?" Francesca repeated.

"But whenever we're in the same room together, I feel this snap, crackle and sizzle." She shook her head. "It's probably all me. Maybe I just want to believe I can have a romantic life after Richard. For so long, I just felt…numb." She paused then went on. "Still, nothing can happen. I'd have to tell him—" She stopped and bit her lip.

"What would you have to tell him?" Tessa asked gently, suspecting Emily needed to reveal something that had been jamming up her emotions for a long time.

Emily finished layering the strawberries, poured a glaze over the top and set the pie in the refrigerator. She took out the pitcher of iced tea. "Anyone want a glass?"

Guessing this was going to be a sit-down conversation, Tessa responded, "Sure." She left the salad fixings on the counter and crossed to the table.

After Francesca ran the chopper, poured the guacamole into a dish and set it in the refrigerator, she did the same. The three women sipped their tea.

Emily stared at the ice cubes in her glass then confessed, "I've been keeping a secret from Doctor Madison."

"Everyone keeps secrets." Tessa realized she'd been keeping one from herself—her feelings for Vince.

"Do you want to tell us?" Francesca asked. "Or is it something you'd rather keep confidential?"

Tessa knew the three of them had become friends because they never pressured each other. They accepted each other just as they were.

"Maybe I should tell you so then you'll understand why I

keep things to myself." Emily turned her glass in a circle then another. "Back in Corpus Christi, I was a midwife who attended home births."

Tessa kept her surprise in check. Home-birthing was controversial. She knew some women preferred it, while other women couldn't afford hospital care and so it was an alternative. But she also knew many obstetricians opposed it and wished they could do away with it altogether.

"I was an obstetrical nurse-practitioner before I became a midwife," Emily continued. "Home-birthing was a need I felt should be addressed and I liked the idea of giving birth to a child in a loving atmosphere with familiar things around, being able to walk and stretch and snack during labor, talk to someone who's a friend as much as a helper in the process. I became friends with my clients. That's what being a midwife was all about for me—making bonds so that a baby comes into the world in the best possible way. I only took on low-risk pregnancies, women who didn't have histories that could cause a problem during labor and delivery. I was good at screening. I also had an obstetrician to back me up and to take over at the hospital if I had to send any of my patients there. In all the deliveries I handled, I only tended to one labor that wasn't predictable. As soon as I saw a problem, I sent her to the hospital. She had a C-section and mom and baby were fine. But then a year later, something I couldn't predict happened. The mother was young, healthy and strong. The dad was there, helping all the way. But when I delivered their little boy, he was stillborn."

"Oh, Emily." Francesca's eyes brimmed with compassion and empathy. As a neonatologist, she saw all kinds of conditions after birth. But at least she had a chance to make them better.

"I'm sorry, Emily, that that happened to you." Tessa covered Emily's hand with hers. "I'm so sorry for the couple."

"They were devastated as any couple would be, and they wanted someone to blame. So they filed a complaint and my license was suspended during the investigation. But they weren't satisfied with that. They filed a civil suit also, and I didn't have malpractice insurance. It's simply unaffordable for nurse-midwives who deliver at home."

"So you had to go through a lawsuit?" Tessa asked, imagining the rigors of it and the emotional impact.

"Yes, I did, and the jury decided there was no malpractice. The autopsy didn't show the cause of death. Unfortunately, that's not unusual. Half of stillborn deaths are still undiagnosed. The licensing board also decided there was no malpractice and I retained my license. But the Wilsons had hired a shark of a lawyer who brought up the other case that had caused problems, insisted I had missed something as a practitioner, that I put the mother and child in danger, that I was only saved by the capable hands of an excellent obstetrician. I was strong at the beginning but as the weeks went by, as articles came and went in the newspaper, as I waited for the licensing board, prepared for the proceedings, paid legal bills out of Richard's pension, I began to wonder. What if I had missed something in both cases?"

"Did you look at the facts?" Tessa prompted.

"I tried to. So much of it was insubstantial. There were questions without answers. And during this, Richard was trying to earn a promotion. He insisted the lawsuit and eventually my attitude toward his job were preventing that from happening. I didn't feel like attending the cocktail parties that are so much a part of what he does, but he didn't understand how I just couldn't put on a mask and pretend everything was fine. A few weeks after the resolution of the lawsuit, he said I was a different person from the woman he'd married. He needed a go-getter, someone who wanted what he wanted, like a huge house and a BMW, a boat and a second home in Boca Raton. I cared about my mothers and babies, the lack of insurance for low-income mothers, the treatment of women in hospitals—all of it. Not material possessions. I guess Richard always cared about money and I just used it for what I needed. I was never an extravagant person. Before and after we married, we had fun together. We had picnics at the beach, concerts in the park, weekends that we wanted to spend together. But then something happened. His job became this all-consuming thing, and it wasn't even the job as much as his determination to climb that success ladder. I think he wants to be CEO someday and that's fine, but he was willing to give up too many important things to get there. I wanted to have children and he kept postponing them, saying when he got the next promotion, that's when we'd do it. But the next promotion was never enough. And now…" She sighed. "I'm writing a check every month to pay him back for the legal fees."

"That was decreed in your divorce settlement?" Francesca asked.

"Richard wanted it, but no, the judge said that shouldn't be expected of me. Yet in a way, it was my liability that caused the whole situation so I feel responsible and I'm paying him back. It'll take years, but I'll do it."

The women sat in silence for a few moments, then Tessa asked, "What's the main reason you don't want Dr. Madison to know?"

"There are lots of reasons. The main one is how many obstetricians view home births. I really don't know how he feels. I never had the courage to bring up that subject. I didn't want to go down that path with him. I guess my main concern is that a complaint was lodged against me and a civil suit. Even though I was cleared of malpractice, there's a cloud that hangs over a professional just with the accusation. That could come into play in so many ways and he might feel he has to fire me. I like working for him. I don't want to have to find another position."

"We'll keep this confidential," Tessa assured her. "You don't have to worry about that."

Francesca nodded. "Absolutely. No one else will know." Francesca reached out and grabbed Emily's hand. "I'm glad you told us. We do all have secrets, and once the secret is shared, it's not a secret anymore. But I think sharing it helps. That's why I told you about my childhood."

"Secrets become a weight that are just too heavy to carry," Tessa agreed.

Emily lifted her glass and took a sip of iced tea. Then she smiled. "A year ago, I would never have believed I'd be sitting around a table with two women I share a house with, drinking iced tea and confiding in them about my life. You two have really helped me find myself again."

"We didn't know you were lost," Tessa joked. "I know both Francesca and I liked you from the moment we met you. That's why we asked you to live with us."

"Maybe I was just hiding." She smiled at the two of them. "So enough about me." She glanced at Francesca. "Are you going to see Grady Fitzgerald again?"

Francesca had told both Emily and Tessa about her encounter with the handsome saddlemaker.

"No. It won't work out. And the truth is, I just don't want a relationship. I want to focus on my career and I don't have time for one. But…" She swerved her gaze to Tessa. "I think *you* might. I heard a little twitter that you visited the moms-and-babies group and that Vince just so happened to be in that group."

"Where do you get your information?" Tessa asked.

"Here, there and everywhere. I also heard one of the moms was smitten with him."

Tessa wrinkled her nose as she remembered Lucy Atkins's interest in Vince. "I didn't stay long."

"Yeah, I heard that, too. Are you going to let her run you off?"

Tessa knew her friend was teasing, but there was an element of truth there, too. "Don't be silly. If Vince wants to start something with someone…" She stopped, realizing she'd better be honest with these two friends. Maybe then she could be honest with herself. "I think *I* want to start something with Vince again, and I keep telling myself I'm absolutely crazy. He's probably not even going to stay here. He hasn't made his decision about that yet."

"And you don't want to abandon your dad to follow Vince somewhere," Emily added. "I can certainly understand that. If my parents were still living, I'd want to live closer to them as they got older."

"Dad and Vince sort of cleared the air over the weekend, as much as they could…though there's no love lost between them."

"They're both twenty years older," Francesca offered. "They've changed. Maybe they'll grow to like each other."

"Maybe, but I'd settle for mutual respect. I don't know what's going to happen tomorrow night with Vince."

"Are you sure about that?" Emily asked with a sly smile.

This was why she'd told them so she'd keep herself honest. "I'm thinking that maybe time with Vince now, even if he leaves, is better than no time at all. I can't keep letting the past get in the way of the present. Or the future."

Francesca stood and raised her iced tea glass. "To us and our friendships. What more do we need?"

Tessa loved her friends, but she was also beginning to realize she needed Vince and Sean in her life, too.

But did *he* need *her?*

"Ready?" Vince asked Tessa as he met her in the second-floor lounge after her rounds.

"Ready. Elevator or stairs?"

They were going two floors up and normally Vince would have suggested the stairs. But tonight he decided, "Let's take the elevator."

After a quiet walk down the corridor, Vince hit the button. He and Tessa stood there, a bit awkwardly he thought. They shouldn't be awkward, but he guessed they were thinking about Amy…and thinking about later.

He was relieved to see no one else occupied the elevator. He and Tessa stepped inside. The doors swooshed shut and the hum of ascension underlined their silence.

"How's your dad?" he asked.

"In a bad mood. I called him at lunch today and he'd had physical therapy. He said his knee hurt—as if he expected it to get better with one session."

Vince smiled. "Of course, he did. He expects his body to do his bidding as most other people in his life do."

Tessa gave him a quick glance.

"I meant in general."

"I know you did."

They both stared straight ahead until Vince blew out a breath. "Are you nervous about tonight?"

She gave him one of those shy smiles that made her look seventeen again. "If I say I'm not, would you believe me?"

"I'll believe what you tell me."

"I'm just not sure where we're headed and—"

The elevator doors opened and Tessa let her sentence trail off as they stepped out.

Vince wanted to step back inside the elevator, hit the button to close the door and kiss Tessa senseless. But he knew this wasn't the time or place.

They were walking down the hall when suddenly one of Amy's friends erupted from her room, yelling, "Get a doctor. She's awake! Her mom says she's awake."

Tessa rushed forward, Vince by her side. When they stepped into the room, they found Amy's mother by her bedside, holding her daughter's hand. Amy was looking around as if she didn't know where she was.

Her mother explained softly, "It's okay, baby. You're in the hospital. You were in an accident." Then her mother ran her hand over Amy's face. "Oh, honey, I'm so glad you came back to us. We were so worried." There were tears in her voice, but happiness, too. So much happiness it filled up the room.

A doctor rushed in from the hall and headed for the teenager. "It's about time you woke up. I think you got enough beauty sleep. Could everyone please leave the room for a few minutes? I'd like to examine our patient."

But Amy's mom wasn't leaving yet. She held her daughter's chin in her palm. "Honey, do you know who I am?"

Amy licked dry lips and seemed unable to form the words at first, but then she nodded, and in a cracked voice said, "Mommy."

When Vince turned to Tessa, he saw the sheen of tears in

her eyes. He couldn't help draping his arm around her shoulders and leading her outside with the others where they spoke to Mrs. Garwin for a few minutes.

Suddenly she put her hand to her mouth. "I have to call my husband. He's working late tonight." Then she hurried down the hall to use the visitors' phone in an alcove. A few minutes later, she was back, tears running down her cheeks. "He's coming right over." She shook Vince's hand and then Tessa's. "Thank you for stopping to see her when you did. I know it helped. I know every visit from everyone helped."

A few minutes later, Vince and Tessa left the group.

"My car's in the parking garage," he said. "Where's yours?"

"Outside the main entrance in the reserved spot."

"Come sit with me for a little while before we leave." He didn't feel as if he wanted to be separated from her yet and she must have felt the same because she nodded and followed him. His SUV was easy to spot. Over the supper hour, visitors had dwindled and fewer vehicles were left.

Vince unlocked the doors with the remote. "Sit with me in the backseat for a few minutes. I want to hold you."

She didn't look surprised and he suspected that she needed to be held. He wondered how often she'd let herself *be* held. If she hadn't had a man in her life in all these years…

After Vince started the SUV and let the air conditioner cool the vehicle, he settled with her in the backseat and tossed his Stetson to the rear compartment. When he wrapped his arm around her, she leaned into him.

He could feel her tremble a bit. "What's wrong?"

"Nothing's wrong. It's just sometimes I think doctors take too much credit for what happens. I think Amy's family brought her back."

"Is this a woman of science I hear talking?" he teased.

"Sometimes there are no explanations, Vince. There was a meeting this morning to discuss putting Amy in another facility. Medical professionals were giving up hope but her family didn't. Thank goodness."

"Thank goodness," Vince murmured into Tessa's temple.

The SUV was warm from the July heat, but Vince knew he was burning up with a fire of another kind, a fire he had to bank until Tessa was ready for it. Still, he dropped his head, nuzzled her nose, found her lips. She kissed him back as if she'd missed him, too. He felt like a teenager, ready to unlatch her bra, ready to lay her back on the seat and take what he hadn't had in twenty years.

But he couldn't just take this time. He had to give.

They were involved in an embrace and a prolonged kiss when Vince's cell phone rang. He thought about ignoring it, he really did, but when he checked the number, he knew he couldn't.

Tessa looked up at him with wide, serious eyes.

"Janet," he mouthed. "I've got to get this." He spoke into the phone. "Janet, hi, I'm at the hospital right now. Yes, I'm headed home. You'd like to come over to see Sean and help put him to bed?" Vince glanced at Tessa. There was disappointment on her face but she gave him a nod.

"Sure, you can do that. I'll be there in about a half hour. I'll pick up takeout and bring it along."

After a "See you soon," Vince closed his phone.

Tessa straightened her blouse and moved away from him. "I should just go home, Vince. I'm sure Janet doesn't want me intruding on her time with Sean."

He gave her a hard look. "You're pulling back again, Tessa."

"I'm not!"

"Anytime we start heating up, you find an excuse to pull away."

Now she moved farther from him, her shoulders becoming rigid. "I'm not the one with excuses, Vince. I'm not going anywhere. More and more I'm getting the feeling that you want to have sex just to see if it's as good as it used to be, not because it will lead us to a serious relationship."

"You make everything complicated," he grumbled.

"Life is complicated and I think you're good at denial. You see only what you want to see. Just what are we starting? A month-long affair. A two-month-long affair? What if the sex isn't as good as you remembered? That maybe I'm not worth the trouble? You're committed to Sean and I admire that, but that doesn't mean you can't commit to someone else, that you can't include more in your life. But for your sake and Sean's and mine, this can't be hit-or-miss. That little boy needs stability. If I begin to get attached to him, and if he attaches to me, what happens if you tear him away? Have you thought about that?"

He really hadn't thought about Sean being attached to her, but she was right, his son would easily become attached to her, maybe already *was*. Sean recognized Tessa when she came into the room. He smiled at her and babbled. He liked her to rock him and play with him. *Was* he in denial? Maybe he was. Because he needed Tessa and he saw that need as simple—just get her into bed and they'd both be satisfied? Get her into bed and the past wouldn't cause the pain it had all these years?

Could Vince commit to staying in Sagebrush when he didn't know if it was where he and Sean belonged? Could he ever be a good husband when he didn't know the meaning of the word? He'd failed before. He couldn't fail again. Sex was only the tip of the iceberg. It was the easiest aspect of their relationship to deal with. But he'd fallen into the trap of thinking it would *solve* something.

He inhaled Tessa's shampoo, her very essence, and wanted her as he'd never wanted her before. Was his needing Tessa worth new yearnings? New risks?

When she moved to the door, he wanted to pull her back. He wanted to hold her and kiss her and explore whatever they needed to explore.

But she was already opening the door to make her exit. "It's probably better if I go home tonight. I think Janet's here for a reason other than to just see Sean. Maybe she'll tell you what that is if I'm not around."

Vince felt as if he were juggling too many balls and one of them was going to fall soon. Spending time alone with Tessa during the week was almost impossible with their long work hours but he wasn't going to just let her walk away. "Are you busy this weekend? I'll have to make an appearance at Sagebrush's Great Chili Cook-off on Saturday. Would you like to go?"

"I have a stint at the first-aid stand from one to two. We could meet after that."

"That sounds good. Do you want me to bring Sean?"

"You know I love spending time with Sean."

"I don't want him to be a buffer," Vince said honestly.

"He's not. He's part of who we are now, together."

Was he? Maybe that's a question Vince had to face. If he and Tessa got together, could she accept Sean as her child? Or would she always long for the boy she'd lost and blame Vince for it?

That was the question they had to answer.

Chapter Eleven

Vince pushed Sean's stroller down Longhorn Way, Sage-brush's main street. He didn't know if it was fitting or not for the chief of police to make his appearance at the Great Chili Cook-off pushing his baby in his stroller, but that's just the way it was. Besides, he'd only be chief of police until the end of the summer.

There were chili stands with burners on both sides of the street. The scent of browned meat, cayenne, chili and onions wafted through the whole town. Hawkers who insisted *their* chili was best had Sean pointing and wiggling and saying "Da, Da, Da" with each step Vince took.

Da Da. The title felt like it fit.

What kind of life would be most nurturing for Sean? There were openings in the Lubbock Police Department, but Vince didn't think that was his best course. With Internet security a priority with most businesses these days, along with security systems themselves, Vince had made a few inquiries and was considering the feasibility of opening his own security firm. But the question was—did he want to stay in Sagebrush? Walking down the street today as chief of police was far different from running these streets as a boy and a teenager and a young man.

"Hey, Chief!" someone yelled from the cover of the barber shop's wooden storefront.

Turning, Vince saw one of his neighbors and waved. Although he was out of uniform, at least half a dozen people had already greeted him by his title. In some cosmic way, that seemed important. After his father had started drinking, no one had respected him. Everyone had known Frank Rossi had fallen apart after his wife left. The downward spiral had happened fast and had never reversed its course. Vince had sworn he'd never let a woman do that to *him*.

Was that the reason he was considering leaving Sagebrush? Because Tessa was here? Because he knew if they were involved seriously again, she would hold the power over him his mother had held over his father?

Was he himself chained to a past he thought he'd escaped?

Vince was tired of the questions, tired of analyzing and second-guessing. He searched for the banner for the first-aid stand and headed toward it.

The first-aid station was covered with a red-and-white canopy, which would be more than protection from the sun, as the weatherman had called for storms later in the day. Tessa stood under one corner of the awning while she ministered to an old-timer who sat on a stool beside her.

She was applying salve to the man's arm. "I heard your chili's the best in Sagebrush, but you've got to be careful."

Tessa turned to take the pack of gauze pads out of the

supply bag and she spotted Vince. The impact of their gazes connecting was almost enough to rock him back on his heels. She broke eye contact first, smiling at Sean.

The old-timer eyed Vince. "So are you going to try my chili, Chief? It's the third stand down from the hardware store."

"I just might do that."

"Maybe we could get some together," a small, feminine voice piped up at Vince's elbow.

He instantly recognized Lucy Atkins's voice. She, too, was pushing her little girl in a stroller.

"I tried to catch up to you, but you were walking way too fast," she continued. "I thought maybe we could get chili together and ice cream for the kids."

Tessa continued to tape the gauze on the old-timer's arm, and Vince could tell nothing from her expression. This was an awkward situation but he knew exactly what *he* wanted. He just wasn't sure about what Tessa wanted.

With his most conciliatory smile, he said to Lucy, "I'm sorry. I made other arrangements to grab something to eat."

Lucy looked at Tessa and back at Vince. "Did I step into the middle of something?"

"Just previous plans," Vince told her casually.

The rattle Lucy's daughter had been holding made a musical sound as she shook it. When she did, it slipped from her fingers, dropping down onto the seat of her stroller. The little girl started to cry.

Vince crouched down and plucked it from the seat, handing it back to her. "Here you go."

Lucy studied him and held his gaze. "Thanks. That's her favorite toy. She wouldn't want to lose it." After another few seconds of awkward silence, Lucy smiled. "The word was out that you came back to Sagebrush as an eligible bachelor. But I've heard other rumors and now I see they might be true. If you ever *are* eligible and want to get together, give me a call. See you next week at playgroup." As she waved, she pushed her baby's stroller away from the first-aid stand.

The old-timer stood up, adjusting his weight on creaky joints. "Looks to me like you've got the best problem there is, Chief—your pick of women."

The old-timer grinned and Vince believed at that point that silence was his best answer.

Thank goodness Francesca broke the awkward scene by running up to the booth. "I'm here to relieve you," she said brightly to Tessa. She dropped down to her knees at Sean's stroller. "And how are you today?"

"Anytime he's in his stroller, he's happy," Vince assured her, keeping his gaze on Tessa. "Are we going to go for that chili?"

"Sure," she agreed with a quick nod. "Just let me get my purse."

After she exited the booth, she sank down to Sean's eye level. "And what would *you* like for supper?"

Sean lifted his arm and reached for Tessa's hair.

She laughed, letting him finger a few of the strands. Then she kissed him on his forehead and pulled away. "I think he likes the idea of ice cream."

"I'll get him real food when we get home."

When Tessa rose to her feet, the breeze ruffled her golden waves. She was wearing a peasant blouse and pink capris. She would be beautiful in a sack. He wanted her with a deep need that unsettled him as much as aroused him.

Tessa walked beside Vince as he pushed the stroller. Being with her this warm afternoon turned back time. He drifted back to afternoons at the lake, stolen kisses at their lockers, hamburgers at the diner.

She didn't say anything as they walked and he asked, "What are you thinking?"

"Nothing important."

"I disagree. When you're quiet, something's on your mind."

She looked down at Sean, hesitated, then replied, "Lucy Atkins obviously wants to connect with you. She's pretty and has an adorable little girl. And…" Tessa hesitated a moment then added, "She could give you more kids."

He stopped walking. "Tessa!" He couldn't entirely keep the exasperation from his tone. "Are you saying you're jealous?" Although the idea gave him some male satisfaction, he also realized Tessa felt an inadequacy that caused her pain.

"I'm embarrassed to admit it, but I guess I am."

Reaching out, he snagged her arm and pulled her toward him. "First of all, I'm not attracted to Lucy the way I'm attracted to you. Second, I'm not looking to have more children. One is enough of a handful. And third, just because she flutters her eyelashes at me, doesn't mean I'm going to take advantage of that interest. I want to spend this evening with *you,* no one else. Am I making myself perfectly clear?"

A bright smile began at the corners of Tessa's mouth and lit her blue eyes.

"Clear," she murmured.

Vince's lips were close to hers. But in a low voice, he insisted, "If I kiss you here, there will be gossip from Sagebrush to Amarillo. So why don't we get that chili and ice cream, take Sean home and feed him and then talk about kissing?"

From the flash of desire that lit up her face, he knew they

were going to do more than talk about kissing. He touched his finger to her lips, then leaned away and pushed Sean's stroller to the nearest chili stand.

In Vince's kitchen an hour later, Tessa watched him wipe Sean's face with a wet paper towel. "That will have to do till we get your bath."

"Can I give him his bath?" she asked, wanting to move on to alone time with Vince, yet feeling the motherly pull toward Sean. She realized how much she loved caring for Vince's son.

Vince smiled. "If you want. Or we can do it together. He likes to splash and is more than a little slippery."

Tessa told herself she shouldn't be nervous. She was in Vince's home with him and they'd spent time here before. But tonight…tonight the current pulsing between them was too strong to ignore. Tonight, she'd have to make the decision about just how involved she wanted to be with Vince…and Sean.

Vince readied Sean's bath, filling a plastic tub within the bigger tub, scattering a few favorite toys around. Tessa prepared Sean and then plopped him into the water. The little boy splashed and giggled and babbled while Vince and Tessa knelt side by side at the tub, their hips bumping, their arms brushing, their laughter mingling. As Vince shampooed Sean's hair and Tessa let water run from a small pitcher to wash away the suds, Sean seemed to love the water. He raised his arm up happily for more. Tessa hoped soon he'd be raising both arms. Physical therapy was helping, but it was slow going.

Vince bumped his shoulder against hers. "I know what you're thinking."

"Now you're a mind reader?"

"No, I can just read the expression on your face. You're hoping Sean will be able to lift both his arms soon."

"I know it can be a long while for the nerves to regenerate. You know that, too."

"Sure I do. But I can't help hoping that he'll heal fast and physical therapy will make him as strong as he needs to be."

Tessa ran her hand down Sean's wet hair. "He's a wonderful little boy."

"Yes, he is," Vince agreed, and looked as if he wanted to say more. But he didn't. "Right now he's a little boy who's getting very sleepy-eyed."

Vince took a huge, fluffy brown towel and lifted Sean out of his tub, wrapping the towel around him. Picking up a second towel, Tessa gently dried the little boy's hair. Her heart felt so light being here with Vince like this, helping to care for Sean. Her hand brushed Vince's chest as she tucked the towel around the little boy and, for a moment, they were both totally aware of each other rather than Sean.

But then Vince stepped away.

Tessa murmured, "I have to get something in my car. I'll be right back."

Vince arched a brow, but she didn't explain further.

Outside, lightning flashed against the black sky, then thunder grumbled. Tessa reached into her backseat for the present she'd bought for Sean this morning.

A few minutes later, she returned to Sean's room, a foot-high blue teddy bear in her arms.

Sean was sitting on his changing table, Vince standing right beside him.

Tessa wiggled the blue bear at him. "How would you like to have a buddy to carry around with you?"

The baby's blue eyes went wide with delight as he reached

for the bear and managed to grab hold of an ear. He flopped the bear up and down, then hugged it with his arm, making excited baby sounds while he did.

"I think he likes it," Vince said with a smile that was all for Tessa and her thoughtfulness. She realized that buying the bear for Sean and giving it to him was a way of welcoming him into her life…and her heart.

As she and Vince dressed Sean, the baby protested when he had to release the bear. He was finally holding it again as Tessa's and Vince's hands bumped into each other while they worked to fasten his diaper and reached for the snaps on his pajama bottoms.

Finally Vince lifted Sean into his arms and held him up high. "Okay, cowboy, time for some shut-eye." He gently laid his son in the crib, the bear settled in a corner, and switched on the mobile.

After Tessa crossed to the crib, she ran her thumb over Sean's smooth cheek and stooped to kiss his forehead. "Nighty-night, cowboy."

She left the room first, her palms a little damp, her heart racing.

Vince switched on the night-light and turned off the overhead. In the living room, he asked her, "Would you like a glass of wine? I bought a peach sangria and a Cabernet Sauvignon. I didn't know which you might like."

But he'd gone to the trouble of thinking about it and choosing two. It made her voice catch a little when she answered, "The sangria sounds nice. Need any help?"

"Nope. While I get the wine, why don't you take a look at the pictures I printed out on the desk? I thought I'd frame a few."

Tessa went to the far corner of the room where Vince's computer sat. It was an up-to-date model with a flat screen, and the printer looked high-tech. Vince had printed out photos from his camera on glossy paper.

"There's a good one there of Sean and Janet," he called from the kitchen. "I thought I'd buy a frame for it and give it to her to take back."

"I'm sure she'd like that." Tessa studied each photo. There was one of Vince and Sean in the backyard. Sean was perched atop the rocking horse that usually sat in his bedroom. It was one of those father-and-son photos that should be kept in a photograph album for a lifetime.

Vince came up behind her. "What do you think?"

She took the glass of wine from him and didn't meet his eyes. "I think they look professional."

"Hard to mess up a photo with a digital camera. I should shoot pictures of you and Sean together."

Unsure what to say to that, Tessa sipped her wine. "This is good."

Vince took the glass from her hand and set it on the desk, then he set his beside it. "I've wanted to kiss you since I saw you at the first-aid stand. But it was too public."

Stroking his fingers through her hair, he drew it away from her face. "I'm aware of the position I hold. I'm aware of your professional reputation. I wouldn't do anything to compromise either."

She knew he wouldn't. Vince's honorable streak was one of the qualities she loved about him.

Loved.

Did she still love Vince as she once had?

"Do you think Sean's asleep yet?" Her voice was husky with emotion.

"He falls off pretty quickly. The baby monitor's on. We'll hear him."

She looked up at Vince and then they weren't talking anymore. He was setting his lips on hers possessively and she found herself wanting to be possessed. No man but Vince had ever interested her. No man but Vince had ever made her realize she was a passionate woman. No man but Vince could make her *feel* as much as she did. She so easily drowned in their mutual desire. His needs fueled hers and she realized there was no decision to make about loving Vince or wanting to be with him.

She wanted Vince.

She hadn't realized that, for all these years, she'd been waiting for him to return. Twenty years ago, they'd developed a bond she'd forced herself to believe had been severed. But she'd been wrong. That bond was still alive and she could deny it no longer.

Vince's kisses became more fevered, his hands more restless as they passed up and down her back. She could feel his heat through his knit shirt and she wanted more of it as his tongue dipped and explored and teased her. After she pulled his shirt up from his waistband, she splayed her hands across his skin.

He pulled back to gaze into her eyes. "You could always make me crazy without half trying."

"Crazy or hungry?" she asked, knowing she was being provocative.

"I need too much when I'm with you, Tessa. That's always unnerved me. Hunger's a part of it, but there's more to it than that."

Now she trailed her fingers around to his stomach, slid her hands into his chest hair under his shirt. "Need isn't a bad thing, Vince."

"Maybe it's not," he decided, taking the hem of her peasant blouse, lifting it up and over her head.

He stared at her for a few moments as if remembering the girl she'd been and comparing that girl to the woman she was today. Her pink bra was a wisp of lace and he easily unfastened it. When he slid the straps from her shoulders, his lips were seductively hot as they kissed under her earlobe, down her neck to her shoulder where the straps had lain. Then he was holding her breasts in his palms. When he brought his lips to one nipple, tongued it then sucked on it, her knees went weak. She braced one hand on the desk to steady her.

"I think it's time we moved to the bedroom." His crooked grin made her insides melt.

Yet he didn't move, didn't try to lead her there. As lightning flashed outside and thunder reverberated in the silence, she realized he was waiting for a response from her. She could still back out. She could leave. She could keep her heart safe. But what was the point of having a heart if she couldn't let it reach for the person she wanted most?

"Make love to me, Vince," she whispered.

He swept her up into his arms and carried her through the living room, down the hall to his bedroom.

Tessa hadn't so much as peeked into Vince's bedroom during her other visits to his house. Now as the light from the hall illuminated it, the heavy pine dresser and king-size bed with its navy and gray comforter barely registered.

He set her by the side of the bed, switched on the table light and turned back the bedding. Then he took off his shirt and tossed it to a chair.

When his hand went to his belt buckle, Tessa covered his fingers with hers. "Let me," she offered, wanting to be a full partner in this, needing Vince to know she wasn't a shy seventeen-year-old virgin anymore.

His belt was stubborn, the leather stiff. She worked at it until it was loose.

When she unsnapped his fly, he sucked in a breath. "If you're going to strip me," he joked, "I'd better pull off my boots."

She waited as he sat on the bed and did just that, then he reached for her, pulling her between his legs, lying back on the bed and taking her with him. His kisses were creative, sensual and so erotic she tingled all over. When she reached inside his fly and cupped his erection, he groaned and rolled her under him. His thighs between hers and his weight on top of her excited her.

This was Vince...her first love...her only love.

Tessa wanted to prolong each kiss, each caress. She re-learned the definition of Vince's muscles and explored his mature male body, relegating the past into the past, appreciating the present and every nuance of the desire they were sharing. They finished stripping off each other's clothes, curious about each new revelation.

When Vince saw the small butterfly tattoo on Tessa's hip, he whistled long and low. "What's this?"

"Rebellion," she replied truthfully. "I got it the day I finished my residency. I guess it symbolized being on my own, trying out my wings."

His lips traced the edges of the tattoo. Then he lifted his head and asked, "How many men have seen this?"

"Vince—"

"How many, Tessa?"

"Only you," she replied softly as rain began a hard rat-a-tat on the roof. Tessa knew as long as she was with Vince, she'd feel safe in *any* storm.

He wrapped her in his arms and kissed her in a way that was demanding and claiming. Their bodies glistened with the give and take of their pleasure until Vince rose above her, slowly entering her. As she received him, Tessa knew fulfillment and satisfaction that had eluded her ever since she was a teenager. Now she was grateful for it, grateful for Vince, grateful for the dream that was unfolding in her heart once more. Her dreams had died when she'd lost their baby…when Vince had left. She'd known she'd become a doctor someday, but that had been a goal, not a dream. Dreams filled with romance and white tulle and babies and parent-teacher meetings and a man who would hold on forever had been blown away like sand in the wind. But tonight, she dared to dream again. She dared to give her heart along with her body. As she and Vince reached for the sublime peak together, as he watched her pleasure and she watched his, as he thrust into her and she asked for more, everything she'd ever wanted seemed to be within her grasp.

They climaxed together and she held on tight, praying this night she and Vince would truly become one.

Vince awakened to the sounds of Sean vocalizing every syllable in his vocabulary. Tessa was cuddled against him, her head on his chest, his arm wrapped around her. If he was honest with himself, last night had unsettled his world. He'd wanted Tessa, no doubt about that. But he'd never expected to need her, not in a way that was all-consuming, exceptional and never-ending.

Was this the way his father had needed his mother? Was this need the reason that her abandonment had driven his dad to find escape in alcohol? If Vince gave in to his feelings for Tessa, what would happen if she left? What would happen if she couldn't accept Sean as her own? What would happen if this time he couldn't figure out how to do it right?

"Should I get him?" Tessa mumbled into Vince's chest.

How easy it would be to share responsibility, to depend on Tessa to parent, too.

"No, I'll get him." Vince moved away from Tessa, conflicted by all of it.

She must have felt an emotional withdrawal as well as his physical one because she pushed herself up onto an elbow and then sat up. "I can start breakfast. Does Sean like scrambled eggs?"

Vince grabbed for his jeans that had landed on the floor last night. "He likes scrambled eggs and little bits of toast with butter."

"That's easy enough," she said brightly, hopping out of bed and finding her clothes, too.

He zipped his fly and was halfway to the door when she asked, "Vince, is everything okay?"

Denial was a hard habit to break. "Everything's fine. By the time you scramble the eggs, Sean will be dressed and ready for his high chair."

Taking a detour from his path out the door, he went to Tessa, kissed her and vividly remembered everything he'd felt while they'd made love last night. But after the kiss, as he left her in the bedroom, he couldn't help trying to make some sense out of his life.

A half hour later, he was sitting at the table with Tessa and Sean, buttering a second piece of toast when his phone rang. After he reached for the cordless phone on the counter, he checked the caller ID. It was Janet.

"Good morning, Janet."

"Oh good, Vince, I got you at home. I'm on my way back from a church service and I wondered if I could stop by. I don't want to intrude on your morning, but it's…important."

He had to remain hospitable, open, friendly. Though the truth was, he was already tired of Sean's great-aunt poking into his life. He hated the feeling that someone was looking over his shoulder and watching every move he made.

"We're just eating breakfast. You can have a cup of coffee with us…or tea."

"I just need to talk to you about something. I won't stay long."

As Vince hung up the phone, he suddenly lost his appetite.

"Janet's coming over?" Tessa asked.

"Yes, she'll be here in a few minutes."

"Do you want me to disappear?"

"No. She can think whatever she wants. All she's going to see is the three of us having breakfast."

Tessa frowned as if she didn't like that answer, but she didn't say anything else, just fed Sean a few more spoonfuls of scrambled eggs.

A short time later, when Janet arrived, Tessa greeted her with a smile then proceeded to load the dishwasher, leaving Vince to make explanations. He didn't really. He just said, "Tessa joined us for breakfast."

After Janet made a fuss over Sean, she took a sheaf of papers from her purse. Looking determined, she handed them to Vince.

"I'd like you to look over those and then sign them."

Vince took the papers, not imagining what they might be. But when he opened them, he saw the heading at the top read Visitation Agreement with the header of a law firm in Lubbock. As he glanced down the first sheet, he read legal mumbo jumbo. The words "weekends every three months" and "two weeks in the summer" leaped out at him. He held on to his temper, knowing that losing it would do no earthly good.

"Why would I ever consider signing these?"

Janet looked nervous but determined. "Because I think

you're a fair man. I think you can understand that I want to be involved in Sean's life. I could go after legal guardianship, you know, saying I could give Sean a more stable life in Santa Fe. But I think he's happy and well cared for with you, and of course, there's the age problem with me. I don't want this to be a fight, Vince. I just want to make sure you don't cut me out of Sean's life."

"You really believe I would do that?"

"Maybe not intentionally. But if you move someplace else, if you're too busy to send pictures, if my visits just aren't convenient for you, I could go six months to a year without seeing him. What I want you to do is think about this, okay? If you do, you'll realize I'm not asking for much. Call me when you've decided."

After a weak smile for Tessa, and a hug and kiss for Sean, Janet exited Vince's condo, leaving silence in her wake.

Vince tossed the papers on the table and swore, muttering, "I'm damned if I do and damned if I don't."

Tessa picked them up, glancing over them. "She isn't asking for a lot of time. This is four weekends a year and two weeks in the summer. It even states that she'll come to you until Sean's old enough to visit her on his own. She named sixteen as a possible age."

"I'll have to see a lawyer," Vince said tersely, feeling trapped, analyzing his options.

"Don't you think it will best if you and Janet figure this out together?"

"She wants me to sign a legal document that affects my life with Sean! Whose side are you on, anyway?"

"I'm on *your* side. But I want you to think about something. If you had family, you might be giving more than this amount of time to *them*."

Vince thought about his dad and how if he were alive, he wouldn't want him anywhere around Sean. He thought about his mother who had deserted them both.

"I don't want to sign an agreement like this."

"Maybe you can negotiate with Janet. Maybe if you assure her you're going to stay in this area…"

Vince held up his hand. "I'm not going to let Janet use a visitation agreement as emotional blackmail, to control what I do or don't do."

Now Tessa's expression changed. Silence vibrated between them until she asked suddenly, "Did last night mean anything to you?"

"Of course it did!"

She set the visitation papers on the table. "You're not acting as if it did. This morning you've pulled away from what we've shared as if you're trying to distance yourself from…us."

Sean began crying to be released from his high chair. Vince felt torn. He wanted to go to Tessa and reassure her, yet his son needed him. Seeing his obvious dilemma, Tessa went to Sean herself, unharnessed him and picked him up.

She laid her cheek against his and told Sean, "I think you and your dad need some time together. I'm going to leave so you can have it." She kissed Sean's forehead and murmured, "But I'm going to miss you," then handed Sean to Vince.

"Don't go. Not like this."

Tessa picked up her purse from the counter. "We both need to think about last night and what it means." Then before Sean could say Da-da again, Tessa left Vince's house, leaving Vince alone in his kitchen…holding his son.

Chapter Twelve

Rain from the late-afternoon thunderstorm that raged through Lubbock poured down in thick sheets onto Tessa's windshield as she headed for the hospital on Tuesday. She was having trouble keeping her mind on her driving. She hadn't seen or heard from Vince since Janet's delivery of the visitation rights agreements a few days ago. She missed Sean, too. So much. She'd been weaving dreams of being his mom—

A stream of water alongside of the road widened and flowed more swiftly. She was focusing her efforts on staying clear of the running water when her cell phone rang.

Tessa pulled her purse onto her lap from the passenger seat.

With her eyes still on the road, she felt for the small phone and pulled it out. As she stole a glance at the number, her heart skipped a beat. It was her facilitator from the adoption agency,

Madalyn Grayson. Tessa told herself not to get excited. Maybe Madalyn just wanted to update material. After all, it had been a few months since the social worker on her case had finished the paperwork to approve her as an acceptable adoptive parent.

She tried to keep her voice steady as she answered the call. "Madalyn! Hi."

"Did I catch you at a bad time? I phoned your office but the receptionist said you'd left for the day."

"I'm in my car on the way to the hospital for rounds. How can I help you?"

"Maybe you'd better pull over."

Madalyn's tone was serious but there was a hint of something else there, too.

"What's going on?"

"*I'm* the one with the questions," Madalyn joked. "Are you ready to be a mother?"

"You're kidding!"

"This has been in the works for a few months, but I couldn't divulge privileged information. Do you remember Angie Marquez and her daughter, Natalie?"

Tessa recalled the young widowed mother and her daughter immediately. But confidentiality held between Tessa and her patients, too. She'd been involved in Natalie's care for a year.

Madalyn jumped back in. "Angie came to us four months ago when she was diagnosed with pancreatic cancer."

Easily Tessa recalled Angie's first visit a little over a year ago when she'd brought month-old Natalie to her for digestive upset. Tessa had switched Natalie to a lactose-free formula and she'd done well. Around three months ago— Natalie had been wearing an Easter bunny on her blouse—

Angie had brought her daughter in again because she thought the baby's ear hurt. Only, Tessa hadn't found anything wrong. Angie had looked as if she'd lost weight but her sunny smile as well as her animated conversation had distracted Tessa as she'd focused on Natalie.

"When Angie saw your profile and video in our selection of parents waiting to adopt, she stopped and didn't look further. She said you related to Natalie as a mother would and Natalie liked you. I think she was so relieved she didn't have to choose a stranger. Call it coincidence. Call it fate. But after she brought Natalie to you again a few months ago, she was sure she was making the right decision."

"Natalie's the baby you have for adoption?"

"Angie died last night. A friend of hers was taking care of Natalie for the past week, but she has three children of her own and can't take on another. Angie took care of all the paperwork before she died. So I just have one question. Are you ready to be a mom?"

Tessa felt overcome with emotion for Angie and Natalie…and for the fact that Angie had chosen *her.* "I'm ready," she replied, her voice catching.

Suddenly she remembered Vince and Sean. What would Vince say about the adoption? What would he think?

She remembered what had happened Sunday, how he felt about Janet's intrusion on his life. She remembered the basis of Janet's worries. Where would Vince be? What would he do? Where would he go? He hadn't called her since Sunday to talk about any of it, to talk about the night they'd shared together, to talk about commitment.

Even beyond her concerns about their night together, she relived that day twenty years ago when Vince came to her father's house and told her he was going to join the Air Force.

Now, he said he'd done it for her. Had he? Now, no matter what she did, would he stay or would he go? Could she trust him to love her? And now, what about this child she wanted to bring into her life?

Years ago, Vince's decision had changed the course of her life. Today, she had to make a decision about this little girl based on what she herself needed and wanted. Natalie needed a mom and Tessa *wanted* to be a mother.

"Madalyn, I want Natalie. When can I get her?"

"I'm glad you're ready for her. You'll have to have a meeting with the judge before you can take her home."

"When?"

"Give us tonight to meet with the lawyers and put everything in order. Come to our office tomorrow morning about nine and I'll go with you to the hearing in the chambers at the courthouse. Hopefully you'll be taking Natalie home with you afterward. Will that work for you?"

Tessa would make it work. "I'll be at your office at nine, Madalyn. Thank you so much."

"No thanks necessary. I'll be giving her over to someone who will be a top-notch mom."

Tessa thought about what had happened to Angie and the heartache she must have experienced. Then Tessa thought about the baby she'd soon be holding in her arms. She almost missed her turn into the hospital's driveway. After she veered into the section of the lot reserved for doctors, she considered again how Vince would react to this turn of events. She had to call him.

First she tried his office. "Sorry, Tessa," Ginny replied. "He's out in the storm, supervising several sites where a storm cell cut through the area yesterday."

"Do you think he'll be checking in?"

"I doubt it. There are downed power lines, uprooted trees. He'll probably just go home and come back to the office in the morning."

After Tessa finished the call with Ginny, she dialed Vince's cell phone. The call wouldn't connect. Because of the storm? She didn't want to phone his home and leave a message…not about this.

She'd try him again later.

Later, after she shopped for some baby supplies. Later, after the idea sank in she was really going to be a mom. Later, after she prepared herself for what Vince might have to say.

Early the following morning, the first thing Tessa did was try to reach Vince *somewhere.* Rhonda told her she'd stayed overnight with Sean because Vince had been on duty all night. At the police department, Ginny informed Tessa that Vince was supervising cleanup in the section of town where the electric lines were down. If Tessa would like, she could leave a message. Finally Tessa left one for Vince at his home and one at his office, as well as on his cell phone, asking him to call her as soon as he could.

She had made a list of everything she needed to buy or do before she brought Natalie home. She was almost in a panic over all of it, when Emily offered her a cup of tea and urged, "Breathe!"

Tessa saw the twinkle in her friend's eyes. Both she and Francesca had been so supportive. "I am breathing," Tessa returned with a laugh. "You just haven't noticed."

Emily poured water from the teapot into a mug. "Today's my day off, too. I'll be glad to run to the store while you're at the courthouse. And before you say another word, I don't mind a bit. This little girl is going to have backup aunties to help out when she needs them."

Emotion caught in Tessa's throat and all she could manage to say was "Thank you."

Emily's hug told her no thanks were necessary.

At nine o'clock on the dot, Tessa's hands were damp as she opened the glass door that led to the second-floor suite of offices. She fidgeted after the receptionist buzzed Madalyn that she was there.

For the past year, she hadn't believed this day would ever come. She hadn't really believed someone would pick her to adopt their child. Then suddenly Madalyn was walking toward her with a beautiful little girl in her arms.

Tessa gazed into the thirteen-month-old's chocolate-brown eyes and felt a perfect fulfillment she'd never known. She took a few steps closer to Natalie. The baby's wide gaze stayed on hers and Tessa's heart burst to overflowing with the love she yearned to give this baby. Reaching out slowly, she almost reverently ran her hand over the little girl's springy brown curls.

Trying to control the emotion in her voice, she opened her arms. "Will you come here, little one? I'm going to be your mommy."

Natalie was silent for several heartbeats and just studied Tessa with those huge eyes. Finally she reached for Tessa, too, and Tessa cuddled her little girl close.

Madalyn smiled, then checked her watch. "I have papers for you to sign before we go to the courthouse."

Tessa passed her hand up and down Natalie's back as the little girl nestled against her shoulder. "And I'll be able to take Natalie home with me afterward?"

"The judge will question you and decide that. But if she's satisfied with everything she sees and hears, she'll award you custody and the adoption process will begin. A social worker will stop in later today or tomorrow to make sure Natalie has everything she needs."

"Do you have a checklist?"

Madalyn cupped Tessa's shoulder. "When she sees the two of you together, I don't think she'll count diapers. Relax, Tessa, and just be the mom you've always wanted to be."

Feeling Natalie resting against her, sure of the rightness of giving this little girl a home, Tessa wished she *could* relax. But she couldn't stop thinking of holding Sean like this...she couldn't stop thinking about Vince.

How would he feel about the decision she'd made?

Tessa was sitting on the couch holding Natalie when the doorbell rang. The little girl was almost asleep, her eyes half-closed, so Emily said, "I'll get it."

Tessa was ready for the social worker. She'd set up a portable crib to the side of the sofa as well as a regular-size one in her room upstairs. She didn't want to be far from Natalie. She needed to give her baby a sense of safety and comfort and intended to stay close.

However, when Emily opened the door a social worker wasn't waiting outside. Vince was!

She heard him say to Emily, "I was on my way to my office and thought I'd stop instead of calling. I saw Tessa's car in the driveway so—"

He stopped short when he saw Tessa ensconced on the sofa, cuddling Natalie.

Tessa gave him a smile that asked for understanding...a smile that hoped he could share her joy.

While Vince just stared, Tessa rose to her feet and laid Natalie in her crib. The baby tucked her thumb into her mouth and didn't awaken.

Emily said in a low voice, "I'll watch her if you and Vince want to go out on the patio to talk."

Tessa asked Vince, "Do you have time?"

"I have time," he agreed, looking wary.

Tessa went through the kitchen and outside to the patio, Vince following.

As they stood on the flagstone, she tried to gather her words, not knowing exactly where to begin. Vince's piercing gaze made her feel as if she'd done something wrong. Yet she knew adopting Natalie was right. "I tried to phone you yesterday when I got the call."

"The call?" His question was curt.

"About eight months ago, I started the screening process with a private adoption agency."

Silence was thick with all of the memories and regrets between them until he asked, "And you didn't think this was important enough to tell me?"

How could she make him understand? How could she explain that if she'd talked about the dream, it could possibly have eluded her? "I didn't think it would ever happen. I didn't think someone would actually choose me."

"Someone did?"

"Yes, she did. Her daughter was one of my patients. Angie's husband was killed in Iraq before Natalie was born. A few months ago, Angie was diagnosed with pancreatic cancer. Neither she nor her husband had family. In fact, Angie's mom and dad were taken from her in an accident when she was twelve, and she was bounced around in foster homes. So she came to the agency where I applied, looking for the right parent for her child for after she was gone. When she saw my profile and recognized me…

"She chose me. *Me,* Vince. I'm actually going to be a mom."

His face took on the stony quality she knew so well when he was trying to hide his emotions. "So what does this mean for us?"

"I don't know what it means for us. After Sunday I wasn't sure there *was* an 'us.'"

He looked uncomfortable. "Because of Janet's visitation agreement?"

"No. Because of your attitude toward it. Toward *me*."

Turning away from her to stare at the horizon, he asked, "What do you want from me, Tessa? My life's in flux because of Sean…because of the temporary job."

Although Vince was there on the patio with her, he seemed so far away. "No, your life's in flux because of *you*. You've always gone after what you want, Vince. You do what you want. You commit to who you want to commit to. Sean came into your life. You wanted that commitment. If you hadn't wanted it, you would have looked into whether or not Janet wanted custody. You said you came back to Sagebrush because the specialist was here in Lubbock, and that's true. But there were specialists other places, too. Why did you *really* come back here?"

He brought his gaze back to hers. "Because Sagebrush was familiar territory. Connections for Sean were easier to make here."

"I came back because my roots were here," she pressed gently.

"I didn't have roots here…nothing to hold on to."

"Memories of *us* are here. Memories of what we could have had, maybe should have had. We found each other again.

What does that mean to you? What did Sunday night mean to you?"

He looked conflicted, as if there were too many doors and he didn't know which one to open. "Twenty years ago, I was committed to us. But *you* weren't. If you had been, you would have come home to our apartment instead of going home to your father."

There it was—the basis of all of Vince's doubts and all his turmoil. He believed she hadn't loved him enough twenty years ago. She hadn't been able to choose him back then, so he believed she wouldn't choose him now.

The pain from the past had caused deep wounds that hadn't healed for either of them. "I made a mistake," she admitted. "I shouldn't have gone home with Dad. But I was certain you were going to come get me. I was certain you were going to come and say, 'She's my wife and she's coming home with me.' I was sure you'd fight for us to be together. Yet you didn't. Instead, you showed up after I left the hospital and told me you were going to join the Air Force. You told me what was best for me just like my father did. You made a unilateral decision and decided our future *without* consulting me."

He shook his head, his expression frustrated and angry. "And that's why you didn't tell me about the adoption? Because now you're making a unilateral decision without me? I think it's more than that, Tessa. You still blame me for everything that happened—losing the baby…your hysterectomy. When I got to the hospital and you were in surgery, your father told me he blamed me and so did you."

"I didn't know he told you that," she murmured, stunned. "I *never* said that."

"Maybe you didn't say it, but I knew you were feeling it. And I think you still are. That's why you can't trust me. If you had trust in me, you would have confided in me. Maybe that's why I didn't look at Sunday night too closely—maybe because I know you're always going to hold my leaving against me and nothing I do or say will change that."

Pain and silence enveloped them both. She could see hurt in Vince's eyes. She could feel it squeezing her heart.

The lump in her throat kept her from speaking as she tried to absorb everything he'd said. Vince's pride had always given him confidence, stature and strength. Now she couldn't miss it descending over him—straightening his shoulders, lifting his jaw, erasing any emotions from his eyes. He didn't say anything as he turned away.

She didn't know what to say to stop him.

He didn't go back through the house but left from the patio. Because he didn't want to see the little girl who had brought the tension between them to a head? He didn't want to be reminded that Tessa couldn't be a mother in the natural way? He didn't want to consider bringing their two worlds together? Possibly one child was enough of a responsibility and he didn't want to consider another. Or was the hurt between them just too great to ever mend?

As Tessa heard Vince's SUV start up, questions raced through her mind faster than she could count them.

Then suddenly none of them mattered. She loved Vince with all her heart. She loved little Sean and yearned to mother him. Maybe in time Vince could forgive her—for what happened in the past…for not confiding in him now. She hoped so. But whether or not Vince could open his heart to her again, Natalie was the one who needed her now.

Tessa hurried to her baby girl, tenderly picked her up from her crib and rocked her in her arms. She didn't stop the tears rolling down her cheeks, knowing she should let them fall. She had to give up one dream for another. It was time to focus on a baby who needed her, not on a man who didn't...who maybe never had.

Chapter Thirteen

"Are you sure I'm holding her right?"

Natalie seemed to be fascinated by Walter McGuire's nose and reached for it. He jostled her a bit so she wouldn't fall out of the crook of his arm onto the sofa beside him.

Tessa sat across the living room from her dad on Saturday evening, marveling at the change in him, at the change in her own life in only a week. She missed Vince desperately. There were so many things she wanted to share with him. She hurt being away from him. At first, she'd checked her phone every hour in case she'd missed his call. But by today, she'd resigned herself to the fact that he wasn't going to call.

"So your practice can do without you for six months?" her dad asked, trying to understand her work situation.

"Six months. Then I'm going back part-time. They found a doctor who was looking to open a solo practice but she decided coming in with a group would have its advantages."

"And you're going to be okay without a salary for six months?"

"I'm fine. Since you footed the bill for my education, I've been saving all these years. I made some good investments."

He gently tugged on one of Natalie's corkscrew curls. "You'll have to start thinking about her education."

"I have a little time."

Natalie grinned at Tessa's dad and swiped at his nose again. He lifted her onto his lap and rubbed his forehead against hers. "You, little girl, are going to be a handful, just like your mother."

When he looked up at Tessa, Tessa almost wanted to cry because her father looked so happy for her.

"You know, I've been thinking," he said. "Maybe I should have this knee fixed. I can't babysit properly if I can't chase her. Looks to me like she'll be walking any day now."

"I know. I also know I'm going to have to make a decision about getting my own place, or staying with Emily and Francesca."

Her dad eyed her above Natalie's head. "As I've told you before, you can always move in here."

"I don't think so, Dad. I love you, but we need our own space."

He scowled at her. "Just as long as you visit often and make this your second home."

"I think as soon as Natalie gets used to the animals, she'll want to be here as often as she can. To see you, too, of course."

He harrumphed, then cleared his throat. "There's an elephant in this room, you know."

Tessa kept quiet.

"You're going to make me ask, aren't you? Okay, I'll ask. What's going on with you and Rossi? You haven't heard from him since you brought Natalie home?"

She really didn't want to get into this with her father. "He obviously doesn't care about me enough to want a life with me. Maybe he never did."

Natalie was tired of just sitting. "Go down," she demanded.

Tessa's father let her swivel from his lap and he moved her to the floor where she crawled to the coffee table, pulled herself up and grinned at them both.

"Good girl," Tessa praised her.

"I think you might have drawn the wrong conclusion," her dad decided, surprising Tessa.

"What do you mean?"

"You pulled one big surprise on the man."

"It was a surprise to me," she murmured.

"You know what I mean. How did you expect him to react when you'd never told him a thing about an adoption? Maybe he thought you took on this adoption to push him away."

Her father's conclusion surprised her. "Since when are you taking Vince's side?"

"I'm not taking sides. I'm just telling you what I see. After you lost your baby, he felt you betrayed him by coming home with me."

Betrayed. She'd never thought about it in those terms before. Had Vince felt betrayed?

"You had something to do with that, didn't you?" She wanted to know if her father would admit his part in it.

"So Rossi finally told you," he said, his cheeks flushing.

"You told him I blamed him for losing the baby!"

"The conditions you were living in—"

"We had love, Dad. You disowned me. Vince took care of me and was doing the best he could. I did *not* blame him. But all these years, he thought I did."

"You proved you blamed him when you chose me over him."

"That was a mistake. A big one."

"And maybe you're making a mistake now by not giving Rossi the benefit of the doubt."

She remained silent.

"When I learned he was coming back here, I looked into his background. He did a damn fine job in the Air Force and he did a damn fine job as a detective. On top of that, he became a father overnight. *Overnight,* Tessa, just like you. And with a child that needed special help. It seems to me he's still finding his way."

"We could have found it together," she said almost to herself.

"Yes, maybe you could have if you'd have told him what you were planning."

She held out her arms to Natalie so the toddler might attempt walking toward her. "But I didn't know if it would happen! I certainly never expected an adoption to happen now."

Her father eyed her and shook his head. "You didn't trust him to understand. Maybe you thought the adoption *would* push him away. Maybe you were scared he didn't have strong enough feelings for *you,* either."

"I don't know what his feelings are. I don't know if he wants me in his life. I won't know unless he tells me. Maybe after we've both had some time—"

"You've had twenty years."

And in those twenty years, Tessa's feelings for Vince had never wavered. She didn't know if she could say the same for his. Yet maybe this time, *she* was the one who had to set her pride aside, to apologize for the hurt she'd caused him. Maybe if she started with a letter…a letter that would explain everything in her heart…

* * *

Vince was sitting on his patio on Sunday afternoon watching Sean as he jumped up and down in his play saucer. His sneakered feet touched the patio and he had as much fun bobbing up and down as he did manipulating the assorted toys around the tray of the saucer.

Vince had been filling his time with lots of paperwork, hours with Sean and nights staring at his ceiling until the sun came up. Missing Tessa was a physical ache. That one night she'd spent with him in his bed had been his idea of perfection. Yet afterward…

"Vince?" Janet Fulton called from the side of the house.

Janet had dropped by twice this past week. The first time *he'd* called *her,* telling her he'd signed the visitation papers and she could come over and pick them up. The second time, she'd brought supper and they'd had dinner and playtime with Sean.

"We're back here, Janet."

She came around the corner, wearing red shorts and a red-and-white-polka-dot short-sleeve blouse. Her running shoes were state-of-the-art.

"Want some company?" she asked, looking hopeful. After another glance at him, she decided, "Never mind. Don't answer that. Are you still not speaking to Tessa? I heard she adopted a little girl. You didn't tell me that," she added quickly.

Right now the benefits of living in a small town didn't outweigh its detriments. "I didn't much feel like talking about it."

Crossing to Sean, Janet crouched down and spun the colorful wheel on his tray. "You have trouble talking about what you feel, don't you?"

Sean's great-aunt had never been anything but polite and casual, except when it came to her great-nephew. But now

Vince had the feeling that was going to change. He ran a hand across his forehead. "Janet—"

"Before you tell me this isn't any of my business, just think about something. You didn't have much family support from what I understand—no mom…a weak father."

"I had an uncle who served in the military," Vince said proudly.

"But he wasn't around much to counsel you, was he? And he died years ago without spending time with you."

"Have you been searching my name on the Internet?" Vince asked evenly.

"Actually, I have," she admitted. "There are articles here, there and everywhere about you. Apparently you made the papers with some heroics when you were a detective."

Vince remained silent.

"Modest and humble like most men who put their life on the line. But I think you have to look at your past to see how it has affected your future. With no family support, you didn't know how to act when you had to face someone like Walter McGuire. You and Tessa fell apart *because* you butted heads with her dad."

"*He* butted heads with *me*. He didn't want me in her life."

"Point noted."

Vince glanced at her sharply.

"Well, whether it was true or not, that's what you thought, so that's what counted. But maybe you should think about what counts now. Do you think I want visitation rights with Sean just to see Sean?"

"You're his great-aunt."

"Yes, I am. But you see, when Scott and Carol died, I lost *my* family, too. Sean might be my only living relative but *you're* his father now. That could make you family to me, too, if you wanted to have family."

Vince had never, ever considered that.

"Family isn't only the people you're given, Vince. Family is what you make of the people in your life. You found that out with Scott. You also found that out with Tessa."

"That was a long time ago."

"Why does it have to be so long ago? Why can't it work now?"

"Because I made too many damn mistakes," he muttered, getting to his feet, pacing across the patio. "She didn't tell me about the adoption because she doesn't trust me. But that's *my* fault. I should have been the one taking care of her after her hysterectomy, after we lost our baby. We should have been holding each other, talking about it, crying together. I made a bad decision by leaving back then. I should have stayed and fought for her, told her father that I deserved her."

"Do you deserve her now?"

The question hung in the afternoon heat until Vince responded, "She might not think so. Seeing Tessa again, being with her again got so out of hand. I didn't realize how much pain was left with the memories, how many regrets we both had. And then the way I acted about the adoption… What a wonderful thing that should have been for her and I acted as if she'd done something wrong."

"This is another regret?"

Now Vince looked at Janet as if she really *were* family. "What if she can't forgive me? For the past, for the mistakes, for acting as if I wanted an affair rather than a life?"

"Maybe you should give her a chance to forgive you so you can find out."

Maybe he should give them both a second chance. For the past week he'd been considering several ways he could do that.

"How would you feel about taking a ride with me and Sean this afternoon?"

"A ride where?"

"To look at some property."

Janet smiled at him. "I think you have a plan."

"I do. Now I'll just have to see if it's going to work."

On Monday evening, Vince came home from work, dressed Sean in his denim overalls, secured him in his car seat and drove to Tessa's. He hadn't called her. He wanted to take her by surprise. That was the best way to get an honest reaction from her. He'd driven by her house and he'd seen her car parked in front so he was pretty sure she was home, along with Emily and Francesca if the vehicles there were any indication.

He didn't care who was there. This was either going to happen or it wasn't going to happen and he had to find out.

With Sean riding on his hip, Vince rang the doorbell of the Victorian, his heart pounding hard.

Francesca opened the door. When she saw him, he could tell she didn't know whether to smile or frown. She glanced over her shoulder to the living room, then in a low voice asked, "Did Tessa know you were coming?"

"No, she didn't. That's the idea. Can I come in?"

Francesca worried her lower lip for a moment then nodded. "She needs to see you."

When Vince entered the living room, he found Emily on the sofa reading a magazine. Tessa was stretched out on the braided rug on the floor, playing with blocks with Natalie.

Tessa spotted Vince and went perfectly still.

Francesca beckoned to Emily and they quickly disappeared into the kitchen.

Recovering her composure, Tessa sat up. She looked beautiful in white shorts and yellow top, her golden hair spilling over her shoulders. He ached to have her in his arms. He ached to share his life with hers.

"I started to write you a letter—" she began.

He raised his hand to stop her words. He wasn't sure he wanted to know what was in that letter. "I came over for a couple of reasons," he began. "Sean and I would like to meet Natalie."

Tessa looked perplexed at his request and then he saw the hope flaring in her blue eyes. He noticed her take a quick breath and swallow hard. Then she scooped up Natalie off the floor and carried her over to him.

At first Natalie lay her head against Tessa's shoulder, obviously shy, maybe even afraid. He was a tall man and he knew that could be intimidating to children. But he smiled at her and said in a gentle voice, "Hello, Natalie. My name's Vince and I brought someone for you to play with. I know he's a little younger than you are, but I think maybe as you get older, you two might be able to have some fun. Natalie, this is Sean. Sean, this is Natalie."

As Natalie eyed Sean from Tessa's shoulder, Vince went on, "Sean had to have a doctor fix his shoulder. His arm still doesn't work very well, but it's getting better. He just needs to be a little careful with it. I thought you should know."

Natalie pushed away from Tessa's chest. "Pway bwocks?"

"Maybe you could teach him to play with blocks. But I thought maybe we could go for a drive first. Would you like us to put your car seat in the backseat with Sean? I want to show your mommy something. I thought you two might like to see it, too."

Natalie stared at Vince for a few moments and then a couple of the words seemed to register with her. "Go. Car."

"I think she got the gist," Tessa said. "Where do you want to take us?"

"I'd like you to be surprised."

Tessa studied him and he held his breath, praying she'd realize how much this drive could mean to them both.

"All right," she replied. "Just let me grab Natalie's bag and I'll be ready."

Ten minutes later, both kids were belted into their car seats in the back of Vince's SUV and Tessa in the front with him.

"Tell me about Natalie," he suggested as they drove. "Is she settling in?"

"She is. At first I was concerned she was going to be withdrawn. She's been through a lot, losing her mom. But I feel us bonding more each day."

"That's what happened with Sean after he came home from the hospital. Day by day we became father and son." He glanced quickly at Tessa and felt a moment of true understanding with her.

Natalie kept a running commentary of things she recognized—cows, cars, a doggie. When Sean babbled, she added, "Sean."

Vince drove east of Sagebrush, past a few developments to a section with individual properties. He pulled up in front of a two-story house with a wraparound porch that needed a good coat of paint. Lots of land surrounded the old house and a For Sale sign stood in the front yard.

"What do you think?" he asked Tessa.

She turned questioning eyes to his. "I don't know what to think."

He unfastened his seat belt and unfastened hers. When she angled toward him, he leaned closer to her and took her hand. "That day in the Sagebrush High School library, I fell in love with you."

He saw her eyes grow moist and knew she was remembering, too.

"That love grew stronger each day I knew you." He squeezed her hand gently. "I've made so many mistakes where you're concerned. I should have gone to your father and made it clear to him that *I* was the one who was going to take care of you. I should have brought you home and we should have grieved together over the baby we lost. We should have decided on the future together, whether or not I'd go into the Air Force, whether or not you'd go to college. But we didn't."

Her hand was warm in his and her eyes were swimming with tears. He plunged ahead. "I left you and now I'm asking you to forgive me for that. Because I love you, Tessa. You're the only woman I'll ever love and your forgiveness can mean having a life with you or not having a life with you. Will you forgive me?"

During the moments she seemed to have trouble finding her voice, Vince's heart almost raced out of his chest. But then Tessa responded, "Oh, Vince. Yes, I forgive you. I love *you,* too. So much. I should have told you I might adopt. But I was afraid you'd back away…afraid nothing would work out. Since Saturday I've been trying to write all of this down. I was going to send it to you so you could think about it…think about us. I've rewritten it three times, afraid you wouldn't understand how much I do love you and Sean."

"I don't want you to be afraid, not ever. We're going to start over. I want to put an offer on this house, build a barn in the back for horses, but most of all, have a fenced-in yard so Sean and Natalie can play together with the two of us watching over them. Will you and Natalie consider marrying me and Sean, so we can spend the rest of our lives together?"

Tessa's smile was radiant through her tears. "Yes, we'll marry you."

He leaned closer to her, giving her a long, tender, loving kiss.

After he broke away, he glanced into the backseat. Sean and Natalie were babbling and pointing to a jackrabbit that had crossed the yard.

He chuckled.

Tessa looked up at him with love in her eyes and stroked his jaw. "What about your job? If we stay in Sagebrush, are you going to work at the Lubbock P.D.?"

"No. I made a few inquiries this week. When my term is over as chief of police, I'll be joining an investigative and security company in Lubbock."

"You'll be happy there?"

"Yes, I think I will be. I'll be happy anywhere as long as you marry me and we can raise our children together."

Tessa repeated, "Our children."

They came together again for another kiss, filled with the promise of dreams they would make come true…filled with the promise of a lifetime of commitment and love.

* * * * *

Don't miss THE MIDWIFE'S GLASS SLIPPER,
the next book in Karen Rose Smith's miniseries
THE BABY EXPERTS.
Available in May 2009 from Silhouette® Special Edition.

Celebrate 60 years of pure reading
pleasure with Harlequin®!
Silhouette® Romantic Suspense is celebrating
with the glamour-filled, adrenaline-charged series
LOVE IN 60 SECONDS starting in April 2009.

Six stories that promise to bring the
glitz of Las Vegas, the danger of revenge,
the mystery of a missing diamond,
family scandals and ripped-from-the-headlines intrigue.
Get your heart racing as love happens in sixty seconds!

Enjoy a sneak peek of
USA TODAY bestselling author Marie Ferrarella's
THE HEIRESS'S 2-WEEK AFFAIR
Available April 2009
from Silhouette® Romantic Suspense.

Eight years ago Matt Shaffer had vanished out of Natalie Rothchild's life, leaving behind a one-line note tucked under a pillow that had grown cold: *I'm sorry, but this just isn't going to work.*

That was it. No explanation, no real indication of remorse. The note had been as clinical and compassionless as an eviction notice, which, in effect, it had been, Natalie thought as she navigated through the morning traffic. Matt had written the note to evict her from his life.

She'd spent the next two weeks crying, breaking down without warning as she walked down the street, or as she sat staring at a meal she couldn't bring herself to eat.

Candace, she remembered with a bittersweet pang, had tried to get her to go clubbing in order to get her to forget about Matt.

She'd turned her twin down, but she did get her act

together. If Matt didn't think enough of their relationship to try to contact her, to try to make her understand why he'd changed so radically from lover to stranger, then to hell with him. He was dead to her, she resolved. And he'd remained that way.

Until twenty minutes ago.

The adrenaline in her veins kept mounting.

Natalie focused on her driving. Vegas in the daylight wasn't nearly as alluring, as magical and glitzy as it was after dark. Like an aging woman best seen in soft lighting, Vegas's imperfections were all visible in the daylight. Natalie supposed that was why people like her sister didn't like to get up until noon. They lived for the night.

Except that Candace could no longer do that.

The thought brought a fresh, sharp ache with it.

"Damn it, Candy, what a waste," Natalie murmured under her breath.

She pulled up before the Janus casino. One of the three valets currently on duty came to life and made a beeline for her vehicle.

"Welcome to the Janus," the young attendant said cheerfully as he opened her door with a flourish.

"We'll see," she replied solemnly.

As he pulled away with her car, Natalie looked up at the casino's logo. Janus was the Roman god with two faces, one pointed toward the past, the other facing the future. It struck her as rather ironic, given what she was doing here, seeking out someone from her past in order to get answers so that the future could be settled.

The moment she entered the casino, the Vegas phenomena took hold. It was like stepping into a world where time did not matter or even make an appearance. There was only a sense of "now."

Because in Natalie's experience she'd discovered that bartenders knew the inner workings of any establishment they worked for better than anyone else, she made her way to the first bar she saw within the casino.

The bartender in attendance was a gregarious man in his early forties. He had a quick, sexy smile, which was probably one of the main reasons he'd been hired. His name tag identified him as Kevin.

Moving to her end of the bar, Kevin asked, "What'll it be, pretty lady?"

"Information." She saw a dubious look cross his brow. To counter that, she took out her badge. Granted, she wasn't here in an official capacity, but Kevin didn't need to know that. "Were you on duty last night?"

Kevin began to wipe the gleaming black surface of the bar. "You mean during the gala?"

"Yes."

The smile gracing his lips was a satisfied one. Last night had obviously been profitable for him, she judged. "I caught an extra shift."

She took out Candace's photograph and carefully placed it on the bar. "Did you happen to see this woman there?"

The bartender glanced at the picture. Mild interest turned to recognition. "You mean Candace Rothchild? Yeah, she was here, loud and brassy as always. But not for long," he added, looking rather disappointed. There was always a circus when Candace was around, Natalie thought. "She and the boss had at it and then he had our head of security escort her out."

She latched onto the first part of his statement. "They argued? About what?"

He shook his head. "Couldn't tell you. Too far away for anything but body language," he confessed.

"And the head of security?" she asked.

"He got her to leave."

She leaned in over the bar. "Tell me about him."

"Don't know much," the bartender admitted. "Just that his name's Matt Shaffer. Boss flew him in from L.A., where he was head of security for Montgomery Enterprises."

There was no avoiding it, she thought darkly. She was going to have to talk to Matt. The thought left her cold. "Do you know where I can find him right now?"

Kevin glanced at his watch. "He should be in his office. On the second floor, toward the rear." He gave her the numbers of the rooms where the monitors that kept watch over the casino guests as they tried their luck against the house were located.

Taking out a twenty, she placed it on the bar. "Thanks for your help."

Kevin slipped the bill into his vest pocket. "Anytime, lovely lady," he called after her. "Anytime."

She debated going up the stairs, then decided on the elevator. The car that took her up to the second floor was empty. Natalie stepped out of the elevator, looked around to get her bearings and then walked toward the rear of the floor.

"'Into the Valley of Death rode the six hundred,'" she silently recited, digging deep for a line from a poem by Tennyson. Wrapping her hand around a brass handle, she opened one of the glass doors and walked in.

The woman whose desk was closest to the door looked up. "You can't come in here. This is a restricted area."

Natalie already had her ID in her hand and held it up. "I'm looking for Matt Shaffer," she told the woman.

God, even saying his name made her mouth go dry. She was supposed to be over him, to have moved on with her life. What happened?

The woman began to answer her. "He's—"

"Right here."

The deep voice came from behind her. Natalie felt every single nerve ending go on tactical alert at the same moment that all the hairs at the back of her neck stood up. Eight years had passed, but she would have recognized his voice anywhere.

* * * * *

*Why did Matt Shaffer leave
heiress-turned-cop Natalie Rothchild?
What does he know about the
death of Natalie's twin sister?
Come and meet these two reunited lovers and
learn the secrets of the Rothchild family in
THE HEIRESS'S 2-WEEK AFFAIR
by USA TODAY bestselling author
Marie Ferrarella.*

*The first book in Silhouette® Romantic Suspense's
wildly romantic new continuity,*
LOVE IN 60 SECONDS!
Available April 2009.

CELEBRATE
60 YEARS
OF PURE READING PLEASURE
WITH **HARLEQUIN®**!

Look for Silhouette®
Romantic Suspense in April!

Love In 60 Seconds

Bright lights. Big city. Hearts in overdrive.

Silhouette® Romantic Suspense is celebrating
Harlequin's 60th Anniversary with six stories that
promise to bring readers the glitz of Las Vegas,
the danger of revenge, the mystery of a missing
diamond, and family scandals.

Look for the first title, *The Heiress's 2-Week Affair*
by *USA TODAY* bestselling author
Marie Ferrarella, on sale in April!

His 7-Day Fiancée by **Gail Barrett**	May
The 9-Month Bodyguard by **Cindy Dees**	June
Prince Charming for 1 Night by **Nina Bruhns**	July
Her 24-Hour Protector by **Loreth Anne White**	August
5 minutes to Marriage by **Carla Cassidy**	September

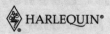

REQUEST YOUR FREE BOOKS!
2 FREE NOVELS PLUS 2 FREE GIFTS!

SPECIAL EDITION®
Life, Love and Family!

YES! Please send me 2 FREE Silhouette Special Edition® novels and my 2 FREE gifts (gifts are worth about $10). After receiving them, if I don't wish to receive any more books, I can return the shipping statement marked "cancel." If I don't cancel, I will receive 6 brand-new novels every month and be billed just $4.24 per book in the U.S. or $4.99 per book in Canada, plus 25¢ shipping and handling per book and applicable taxes, if any*. That's a savings of at least 15% off the cover price! I understand that accepting the 2 free books and gifts places me under no obligation to buy anything. I can always return a shipment and cancel at any time. Even if I never buy another book from Silhouette, the two free books and gifts are mine to keep forever.

235 SDN EEYU   335 SDN EEY6

Name _____ (PLEASE PRINT) _____

Address _____ Apt. # _____

City _____ State/Prov. _____ Zip/Postal Code _____

Signature (if under 18, a parent or guardian must sign)

Mail to the **Silhouette Reader Service:**
IN U.S.A.: P.O. Box 1867, Buffalo, NY 14240-1867
IN CANADA: P.O. Box 609, Fort Erie, Ontario L2A 5X3

Not valid to current subscribers of Silhouette Special Edition books.

Want to try two free books from another line?
Call 1-800-873-8635 or visit www.morefreebooks.com.

* Terms and prices subject to change without notice. N.Y. residents add applicable sales tax. Canadian residents will be charged applicable provincial taxes and GST. Offer not valid in Quebec. This offer is limited to one order per household. All orders subject to approval. Credit or debit balances in a customer's account(s) may be offset by any other outstanding balance owed by or to the customer. Please allow 4 to 6 weeks for delivery. Offer available while quantities last.

Your Privacy: Silhouette is committed to protecting your privacy. Our Privacy Policy is available online at www.eHarlequin.com or upon request from the Reader Service. From time to time we make our lists of customers available to reputable third parties who may have a product or service of interest to you. If you would prefer we not share your name and address, please check here. ☐

SSE08R

The Inside Romance newsletter has a NEW look for the new year!

Same great content, brand-new look!

The Inside Romance newsletter is a FREE quarterly newsletter highlighting our upcoming series releases and promotions!

Click on the Inside Romance link on the front page of **www.eHarlequin.com** or e-mail us at insideromance@harlequin.ca to sign up to receive your FREE newsletter today!

You can also subscribe by writing to us at: HARLEQUIN BOOKS Attention: Customer Service Department P.O. Box 9057, Buffalo, NY 14269-9057

Please allow 4-6 weeks for delivery of the first issue by mail.

Silhouette®

COMING NEXT MONTH

Available March 31, 2009

#1963 THE BRAVO BACHELOR—Christine Rimmer
Bravo Family Ties
For attorney Gabe Bravo, sweet-talking young widow
Mary Hofstetter into selling her ranch to BravoCorp should have
been a cinch. But the stubborn mom turned the tables and got him
to bargain away his bachelorhood instead!

#1964 A REAL LIVE COWBOY—Judy Duarte
Fortunes of Texas: Return to Red Rock
CEO William "J.R." Fortune gave up the L.A. fast life to pursue
his dream of becoming a Texas rancher. Luckily, hiring decorator
and Red Rock native Isabella Mendoza to spruce up his new spread
ensured he'd get a very warm welcome in his brand-new life!

#1965 A WEAVER WEDDING—Allison Leigh
Famous Families
A one-night stand with Axel Clay left Tara Browning pregnant.
But when she was forced to share very close quarters with the sexy
bodyguard, would she end up with a love to last a lifetime?

#1966 HEALING THE M.D.'S HEART—Nicole Foster
The Brothers of Rancho Pintada
To help his sick son, Duran Forrester would do anything—including
a road trip to Rancho Pintada to find the long-lost family who might
hold the key to a cure. But first, he crossed paths with pediatrician
Lia Kerrigan, who had a little TLC for father and son alike....

#1967 THE RANCHER & THE RELUCTANT PRINCESS—Christine Flynn
After her unscripted remarks blew up in the tabloids, Princess Sophie
of Valdovia needed to cool off out of the public eye in middle-of-
nowhere Montana. But that's where things heated up—royally—with
rancher and single dad Carter McLeod....

#1968 THE FAMILY HE WANTED—Karen Sandler
Fostering Family
Bestselling novelist Sam Harrison had it all—so why did the former
foster kid-made-good feel so empty inside? The answer came when
old friend Jana McPartland showed up on his porch, pregnant and in
distress, and he realized that it was family he wanted...and family he
was about to find.